Once Upon a Thriller

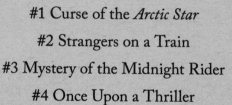

NANCY DREW DIARIES™

Once Upon a Thriller

#4

CAROLYN KEENE

Aladdin
NEW YORK LONDON TORONTO SYDNEY NEW DELHI

This book is a work of fiction. Any references to historical events, real people, or real places are used fictitiously. Other names, characters, places, and events are the product of the author's imagination, and any resemblance to actual events or places or persons, living or dead, is entirely coincidental.

ALADDIN

An imprint of Simon & Schuster Children's Publishing Division

1230 Avenue of the Americas, New York, NY 10020

First Aladdin paperback edition September 2013

Copyright © 2013 by Simon & Schuster

ALADDIN is a trademark of Simon & Schuster, Inc., and related logo is a registered trademark of Simon & Schuster, Inc.

Also available in an Aladdin hardcover edition.

For information about special discounts for bulk purchases, please contact Simon & Schuster Special Sales at 1-866-506-1949 or business@simonandschuster.com.

The Simon & Schuster Speakers Bureau can bring authors to your live event. For more information or to book an event contact the Simon & Schuster Speakers Bureau at 1-866-248-3049 or visit our website at www.simonspeakers.com.

Designed by Karina Granda

The text of this book was set in Adobe Caslon Pro.

Manufactured in the United States of America 1113 OFF

2 4 6 8 10 9 7 5 3

Library of Congress Control Number 2013944613

ISBN 978-1-4169-9074-1 (pbk)

ISBN 978-1-4424-6612-8 (hc)

ISBN 978-1-4424-6572-5 (eBook)

Contents

Dear Diary,

IT'S NO SURPRISE THAT MY NOSE IS always stuck in a book. I can't get enough of a good biography, historical novel, or fantasy story. But my favorites are edge-of-your-seat, page-turning mystery stories. And when Bess, George, and I were in the middle of a raging storm on Moon Lake, I wished I were just reading a mystery, not smack in the middle of one.

CHAPTER ONE

Burned

"COME ON. HURRY UP AND LET'S GO!" I called to Bess and George as I popped open the trunk of my car. I had parked in front of George's house and was in a rush to get going.

"Leave it to you to be right on time, Nancy," Bess teased as she and George walked down the front steps of the porch and headed toward me, overnight bags in hand. George glanced at her watch.

"Whoa, Bess is right!" George said. "It's nine a.m. on the dot." She grabbed Bess's bag and tossed it and her own into the trunk before slamming it shut.

"Well, that's when I told you I'd be here," I answered. "And I'm really looking forward to getting to the lake early so we can settle into our cabin and go for a hike before it gets too hot."

"Ugh," Bess groaned. "Not a hike! You and George promised me this would be a relaxing weekend."

"And it will be," I said. "A short hike this morning, followed by a canoe ride this afternoon. Then tomorrow we can sleep in and read and relax before we go waterskiing after lunch."

Bess rolled her eyes at me. I could tell she would have preferred spending the entire weekend doing nothing but sitting on the shores of Moon Lake with a magazine and a bottle of nail polish to touch up her manicure and pedicure. But there's no way I could manage that—I would get way too antsy.

Besides the outdoor activities, I also planned to read the latest Miles Whitmore mystery, *Terror on the Trail*. Lately, I couldn't get enough of his books. I never figured out "whodunit" till the very end, and I'm an amateur detective. That's how crafty a writer he is.

I pulled away from George's house and maneuvered my car toward the highway. Once we got going, it was only about fifty miles to Avondale, which is where Moon Lake is located. If we didn't hit any traffic, we'd be there in under an hour.

"We'll make it up to you, Bess," George said. "You have complete control over music for the entire weekend."

"Really?" Bess asked, incredulous. "I'm not sure I believe you. You always hate any group I like."

"Really. I promise," George said. I was impressed. George can be incredibly opinionated when it comes to music. She and Bess are my best friends, and they also happen to be cousins. But the two are as different as Beethoven and The Rolling Stones. Sometimes it's hard to believe they're related.

"Well, I suppose that's something," Bess said with a sigh. She plugged her MP3 into the radio and out blasted Grayson & James, her latest favorite group.

I saw George in the rearview mirror, and I knew she was working hard to restrain herself. I saw her putting on her own headphones to drown out Bess's music.

"I know, I know," Bess half apologized, sensing George's frustration. "But this is great driving music, isn't it, Nancy?"

"I actually like this song," I admitted sheepishly. I was trying to keep the peace between my friends, but I was also being truthful—the song was catchy and fun. And with that, we all settled in to enjoy the ride.

We pulled up to our rental cabin on Moon Lake almost exactly an hour later. Towering green pines surrounded the cabin, and the setting looked inviting. I couldn't wait to get started—within minutes, the car was unpacked and our hiking boots were on.

"I promise it will be a short hike, Bess," I told her as I pulled my hair into a tight ponytail. "Let's just do one loop around the lake. We'll be back in time for lunch."

"All right," Bess grumbled. "Let's get this over with." She tightened the laces on her boots and the three of us headed for the trailhead, which happened to be just a few paces from our cabin.

As we hiked, I took in the beautiful scenery and

tried to let my mind wander. That can be tough for me, as I always have some mystery on my mind—a real one or one in a book.

But this weekend at the lake I really planned to focus on my friends and the great outdoors.

"Right, Nancy?" I heard George say. She was looking at me as though she'd been talking to me for five minutes without a response. Which, come to think of it, was quite possible.

"Oh, uh, sorry, George," I replied. "I guess I was lost in my own world."

"I said, that's our cabin right there, isn't it?" George repeated, pointing to the little wooden structure peeking through the trees a few hundred yards ahead of us.

"It is," I replied, glancing at my watch. "Wow, that was quick." It had taken us less than an hour to hike the three-mile loop around the lake. Even Bess agreed that it had been pleasant and not particularly taxing.

"Great!" George said. "Because I'm ready for Hannah's lunch."

Back at the cabin, I went into the kitchen to get the

basket Hannah had packed for our weekend. Hannah Gruen is my dad's housekeeper, and she loves to keep all of us well fed and nurtured—she's got lots of love to share. I couldn't wait to dig into some of her famous fried chicken and homemade coleslaw.

But the basket was nowhere to be found. Suddenly an image of it popped into my head. It was sitting on the counter—the counter at my house in River Heights, that is.

"Bad news," I groaned. "I left the lunch basket Hannah packed for us at home."

"That's because you were rushing like crazy to get up here," George said. "What's my stomach supposed to do?" she joked.

Bess smiled broadly. "I guess we'll just have to make a trip into town, then," she suggested. "It's not far away, and I'm pretty sure Avondale has a bunch of cafés and cute stores."

She emphasized the word "stores," and knowing Bess, she was eager to squeeze in some shopping along with lunch.

"Great," I agreed. "Because I also left *Terror on the Trail* at home, so now I have nothing to read. Hopefully there's a bookstore in town too."

"Terror on the what?" George asked. "Do you ever stop trying to solve mysteries?" She tapped her tablet, which was perched on a nightstand. "You know, Nancy," she continued, "you wouldn't have this problem if you weren't so resistant to e-books. You could take ten books with you at once."

"As long as she remembered to actually bring the reader," Bess pointed out.

"Ha, ha," I said drily. "But you know what? When it comes to books, I like the feel of the pages in my hands, and even the smell of them."

"That's Nancy," George teased. "Always with her nose in a book—literally. Now let's go—I'm starving!"

Ten minutes later we pulled into the town of Avondale. And Bess was right—there were plenty of quaint stores and shops. But that's not what caught my attention. Two fire trucks were stopped in the middle of the street, and an acrid smell filled the air.

We parked and quickly made our way toward the crowd that had formed.

"Was there a fire?" I asked a man with a golden retriever close by his side.

"Looks that way," he replied, shaking his head and gesturing toward a nearby building. A sign in front of the shop was in the shape of an open book. "And at Paige's Pages, of all places."

Nearby, three young women had their heads together, whispering—but loud enough that we could hear them.

"And now we won't get to meet Lacey O'Brien," one of them said.

"I can't believe it, Carly!" another replied. "And I've read all her mysteries."

That word got my attention. I moved closer to the girls.

"Excuse me," I said. "Do you know what happened? We're just here for the weekend, but what's going on here? I was trying to get to the bookstore,

but it looks like that's going to be, uh, difficult."

"We were here for the bookstore too," the first girl replied. "Lacey O'Brien was supposed to do a reading and a book signing—you know, the mystery writer?"

"I've heard of her, sure," I replied.

"She's like a local celebrity around here," the second girl, who had dark, curly hair, said. "Well, except that people hardly ever see her. I heard this book signing was the only one she was doing all year."

"And now we're out of luck, aren't we, Mandy?" the third girl added. "No signing today."

The girls continued chattering, and I took a few steps back. But I could still hear them clearly. In fact, everyone around us could. A firefighter near us was talking with a distraught-looking woman with graying hair who was pointing to the store.

"Did you realize there was a fire in her latest book, *Burned*?" Mandy whisper-shouted to her friends.

"You're right!" Carly answered. "That's a weird coincidence. You don't think Lacey had anything to do with this fire, do you?"

"Well, at least something finally happened here. Nothing exciting or mysterious ever happens in Avondale," Mandy said.

I wouldn't be so sure, I thought. That's what everyone thinks until something actually happens.

At that moment, one of the other firefighters approached us.

"Everyone, please step back," he announced. "We need to get our equipment out of the store."

"Sure, no problem," George said. We all moved back, but Mandy had ideas of her own and went right up to the fireman.

"What happened?" she demanded. "We really, really wanted to see Lacey O'Brien today. And now we might have to wait another year until we do."

I could have sworn the fireman rolled his eyes. But he patiently answered her question. "From our initial investigation, it looks like some faulty wiring in an old chandelier," he replied. "That happens a lot in older buildings like this one."

Mandy gasped. "It does?" she asked, an amazed

look on her face. "Because that's exactly how the fire started in Lacey O'Brien's last book! Except the wiring in the chandelier hadn't really caused the fire. It was arson!"

CHAPTER TWO

The Missing Wallet

I TURNED TO GEORGE AND BESS TO SEE if they had been listening. One glance at their faces told me they had heard everything. In fact, there was an almost collective gasp from the crowd around us.

"Hmm," the firefighter replied. "That's very interesting. But until we do a more complete investigation, we can't make that assumption, miss."

Mandy turned back to her friends. "Well, I can, and I will," she whispered to them.

The crowd broke up and Bess, George, and I walked slowly down the main street.

George cleared her throat. "Nancy, if this is arson, then it's really none of our business, right?" she began. "We can just go about our weekend plans, can't we?"

"Without you looking under every rock," Bess chimed in.

My mouth dropped open, but I wasn't really surprised. My friends knew me better than anyone, except maybe for Ned. And they knew it would be close to impossible for me to resist a suspicious fire and a well-known writer who happened to specialize in mysteries.

"I guess I'm an open book," I agreed with a soft laugh. "No pun intended."

"Well, before we start," George said as we walked, "can we grab some lunch first? I won't be much help unless I eat."

"Why don't you and Bess find someplace, while I ask a few more questions? Just text me where you go, and I'll meet you there in about ten minutes. Okay?" I said.

"Perfect," George agreed as she and Bess headed down the street.

I turned back toward the spot where the firefighter had been talking with Lacey O'Brien's fans. Most everyone who had gathered was gone, except for the firefighter who Mandy had questioned. He was busy talking on his phone and I waited a moment until he seemed like he was wrapping up his conversation.

"Excuse me," I asked. "But do you know when the bookstore might reopen? And when Lacey O'Brien will be signing her books?"

"I think you're out of luck," he replied. "The store won't be reopening for a few weeks at least. It wasn't a bad fire, but there's a lot of smoke and water damage. The owner, Paige Samuels, has quite a mess on her hands."

"Do you think those girls were right?" I asked innocently. Then I thought fast. "My brother's a volunteer firefighter and has never dealt with arson before."

"I really don't know and can't say just yet," he replied. "It looked like bad wiring to begin with, but it could have been anything. As I said, we'll be doing a full investigation, but it's too soon to tell right now."

He excused himself and headed over to the other firefighters. I nodded and backed away. Then I pulled out my phone to see if George or Bess had texted me. I had one new message from George: MEET US AT THE AVONDALE DINER, CORNER OF PARKSIDE AND MAIN.

I headed up the street, passing an eyeglasses store and a bakery. Baskets of purple and pink impatiens hung from the streetlamps, and I had the feeling that Mandy was probably right that nothing exciting ever did happen in Avondale. It was quiet and quaint with a small-town feel. So why now—why a fire? And who? And did the fire really have anything to do with Lacey O'Brien's book? Or maybe even Lacey O'Brien herself?

At that moment I passed the Cheshire Cat Inn. In front a woman was sweeping the sidewalk, mumbling to herself. She had curly, dark-brown hair with a distinctive streak of gray in it. As I got closer, I realized she was talking to someone—an older man in an apron who stood half-hidden in the doorway to the bakery.

"She had it coming to her, if you ask me, Arnold," I heard her say.

"Now, now, Alice," the man scolded gently. "I know you and Paige have never been the best of friends, but no one deserves to have her shop practically burned to the ground."

I couldn't believe my luck. They were talking about the bookstore and the owner. I had to find out more.

"I'm sorry to interrupt," I said. "But I think I'm a bit lost. Is this the way to the Avondale Diner? Parkside and Main?"

"You're going in the right direction," the man— Arnold—replied. "This is Main Street here. Just keep walking two more short blocks and you'll come to Parkside. The diner's on the other side of the street. Best peach pie around, by the way," he added, and smiled.

"Thank you," I said, and started walking, but then turned back.

"One more thing. I was hoping to get a copy of Lacey O'Brien's latest mystery at the bookstore, but her signing was canceled." I gestured toward the few people still lingering in front of Paige's Pages. "Do either of you know of another place in town that sells books?"

The woman stopped sweeping. "I sell all of Ce—I mean, Lacey's—novels in my gift shop," she replied, somewhat too cheerily. She stepped into the lobby of the inn and motioned for me to follow her.

"Thanks, that's perfect," I said. I followed her into the lobby, which was dim, dark, and covered in ornate, flowery wallpaper. An enormous antique grandfather clock stood against one wall. Just beyond it was a small arched entryway that led to a tiny nook of a room. In addition to a wide variety of antiques, it was packed with Cheshire cat–themed gifts, from salt and pepper shakers to clocks to tea towels and Alice in Wonderland books and toys.

"This is a lovely place," I said as I studied an antique Tiffany lamp in the entryway to the gift shop. "It's so charming."

"Thank you," she answered. She seemed surprised at the compliment. "It's nice to see a young person like yourself appreciates dusty old antiques the same way I do. Most girls your age are more interested in cell phones and technical gadgets." She wrinkled her nose in disgust. "I'm Alice Ann Marple, by the way. Lacey O'Brien's from around here, you know. Tourists know she's a local writer, so guests are always asking for her books."

"Nice to meet you. I'm Nancy Drew," I said. "I'm a writer myself," I fibbed. "And a big mystery fan." I gestured to the rack of Lacey O'Brien's novels, which was tucked between a display of antique picture frames and a shelf of cat figurines. There were at least ten different titles to choose from.

"I'm sure you know, but this one's her latest," Alice Ann began, picking up a copy of *Burned*. The front cover showed an old house lit up in bright flames. "But this one's my favorite."

She handed me a copy of a book called *Framed*, which had an image of a shadowy figure in an oversize picture frame on the cover.

"You know, all of her books are set in a town that's similar to Avondale," Alice Ann continued. "Some people even think they're based on real crimes, but I think that's just ridiculous. I went to high school with her, and she had quite an active imagination."

What was Alice Ann saying? Did she know something about the fire today? "Are you still close friends?" I asked.

"Friends? Close?" Alice Ann scoffed. "We were never really close. I wouldn't even say we were friends. We were foe—" Alice stopped. And then she went on but in a more measured tone. "Lacey was—well, she kept to herself. Still does, as a matter of fact."

I nodded. "Well, it would have been nice to see Lacey today, especially since I hear she rarely makes public appearances to promote her books. And how awful about the fire. I really feel bad for the owner." I hoped Alice would continue talking about Paige.

But she just gave me a tight-lipped nod. It seemed like she had remembered that I was a stranger in town and not an old acquaintance to gossip with. I guessed I wasn't going to find out why Alice felt Paige had something coming to her.

"Yes, it's quite a tragedy," she replied. For a moment

I thought I heard sarcasm in her voice, but I couldn't be sure because she moved on.

"Have you decided on a book?" she asked, gesturing to the two paperbacks I was holding.

"I'll take them both," I replied. "Thanks again for the help."

"Of course," she said. "I'll ring them up for you." It was clear our chat was over.

A few minutes later I was sitting in a booth at the diner with George and Bess, who were finishing dessert.

"We almost started to worry about you," Bess said. "But we went ahead and ordered you an avocado-and-cheddar wrap with hummus. Hope that's okay."

"Well, it's not Hannah's fried chicken, but it still sounds pretty good," I replied. "I'm starving."

"So, what did you find out?" George asked.

"Only that Lacey O'Brien grew up here and keeps to herself, and that Alice Ann Marple, owner of the Cheshire Cat Inn, is no fan of Paige Samuels or Lacey

O'Brien. I overheard Alice saying that Paige had it coming to her, and then she started to say that she and Lacey were more enemies than friends." I knew it would be way too easy if Alice Ann was the one to set the fire, but what did she mean by her remarks?

I took a sip of water from the glass in front of me.

"And I bought two Lacey O'Brien books," I said. I pulled out my copies of *Burned* and *Framed*.

"Nice work," George said. "Why don't you give me *Burned* and you take *Framed*, and we'll see if there's anything to what those girls said about the bookstore fire."

"Well, it's a first step at least," I said. "But I think we're just getting started. You don't think *she* could have been behind the fire, do you?"

Bess started to answer, but the waitress arrived with my wrap, and as she placed it on the table, she noticed my books.

"I loved *Burned*. I think it was her best yet," she commented.

"I just started it, but so far it's terrific," I agreed.

"Lacey O'Brien lives in town, right?" Bess asked innocently. "Does she ever eat here?"

"Never has on any of my shifts," the waitress replied. "She doesn't live in town, though—she has a cabin on Moon Lake. And she's one of those reclusive writer types. She does one signing a year at Paige's Pages, but that's it. No one around here sees her for the rest of the year."

So the girls who we saw at the fire and Alice were in agreement about Lacey—she really didn't show up in town often.

"We're staying in a cabin on the lake. Maybe we'll bump into her up there," Bess said to the waitress.

"You never know," she said with a shrug. "But her cabin is almost completely hidden. You can't even see the place from the road. I've heard that her lakefront is decorated with a huge carving of a brown bear. I've never seen it myself, but that's what a customer told me."

Then the waitress leaned into our table and said, "I don't think folks from around here like her too much.

Like she thinks she's better than everyone who lives in Avondale."

She tucked the check under the saltshaker and moved on to take the order of the couple seated at the table behind ours.

"Wow," Bess whispered. "I wonder what she meant by that. And I'm totally intrigued by this hidden cabin."

"And the bear," George said. "That's a great way for us to find the cabin from the lake."

"If we could score an interview with Lacey O'Brien, that would be terrific," I remarked.

George nodded. "We can still take the canoe out this afternoon," she suggested. "Maybe, just maybe, we'll be able to spot that bear and Lacey's cabin."

"Sounds like a plan," I said as I picked up the check. "By the way, lunch is on me."

I opened my backpack and reached inside for my wallet.

Then I gasped.

"What is it?" Bess exclaimed.

"My wallet," I groaned. "It's gone!"

CHAPTER THREE

Capsized!

"I THOUGHT NOTHING EVER HAPPENED in Avondale!" George cried. "First a fire and now a lost wallet? Did we bring this bad luck with us?"

"Oh no," Bess said. "Do you think it was stolen?"

"Anything's possible," I said, sighing and searching through my backpack again. "I hope not. I'll have to cancel all my credit cards and get a new license. What a pain!"

"When did you last have it?" George asked, not wasting a second.

It took me a moment to retrace my steps, but it came to me pretty quickly.

"The Cheshire Cat," I said. "At the gift shop."

"Oh, is that where you bought the books?" Bess asked.

I nodded, breathing a sigh of relief as I pointed to the novels still sitting on the table. My wallet probably hadn't been stolen—more likely I had flaked out and left it on the counter while talking to Alice Ann.

"Let's go. We'll stop there on the way back to the car," George said as she went to pay the bill.

"Thanks, George." I smiled. For someone with such a great memory when it came to mysteries and clues, I could sometimes be surprisingly absentminded about everyday things like wallets and car keys.

As soon as we entered the inn, Alice Ann cried out, "I'm so glad you came back! You left your wallet on the counter when you paid for those books. I've been waiting for our front desk clerk to return from her lunch break so I could dash up to the diner to return it to you."

"Thanks so much," I said, relieved. "I can be such a scatterbrain sometimes."

"Happy to help," Alice Ann replied. Then she noticed George and Bess behind me. "I didn't know you had friends with you. Any chance you need a place to stay? We've had a few cancellations, so there's plenty of room here at the Cheshire Cat."

"No thanks," Bess said. "We've already rented a cabin on the lake."

Suddenly I had an idea. Maybe I could get Alice Ann to open up a bit more after all.

"Speaking of the lake, the waitress at the diner mentioned that Lacey O'Brien lives up there," I began. "I know you said she keeps to herself, but any chance you know which cabin is hers? Of course, we wouldn't bother her, but we're taking a canoe ride this afternoon, and it might be fun to just pass by."

Alice Ann hesitated for a moment.

"Well, I'm not in the habit of advertising her whereabouts to tourists," she said. "We may not have ever been close friends, but I suppose the woman is entitled to her privacy."

She paused again. I waited, sensing that she was about to give in.

"Well, I suppose it won't do any harm . . . but hers is the cabin on the northwest corner of the lake. And you won't be able to miss it from the water because there's a massive carving of a grizzly bear on the shore. That monstrosity must have cost her a fortune," Alice said, and pursed her lips. "I don't know what she was thinking when she commissioned that piece."

"Ummm . . . thank you, Alice. We'll just paddle by and get a peek at the place from afar," I told her, knowing full well that Bess, George, and I had other plans.

Alice Ann nodded curtly. Once again she was acting as though she might have opened up and said too much.

"You enjoy your books, now," she said as we thanked her again and headed back out the door and to the car.

On our way back to the cabin, we stopped at a grocery store to pick up a few supplies. Bess headed to the produce aisle for fruit and vegetables, while George and I picked up some bread, cereal, and milk for breakfast the next morning.

The three of us met in the checkout line. We were right behind a nervous and tired-looking woman who was speaking with the checkout clerk in hushed tones.

"—so sorry about the fire, Paige," I heard the clerk tell the woman.

With a start, I realized we were behind Paige Samuels, the owner of the bookstore! I glanced quickly at the items she was purchasing, which included a box of heavy-duty trash bags, a large flashlight, a heap of batteries, and a case of bottled water. Then I elbowed George in the side and silently gestured to the woman. George glanced at the supplies and gave me a quick nod, and we both leaned in a bit to hear more.

"Thank you," Paige said to the cashier in a quiet voice. "It's quite a shock."

"Do you know what happened?" the clerk replied. "A few people have said that it might have been arson. What do you think?"

Paige seemed surprised by the suggestion. "No,

no," she replied hastily. "The building is very old, you know. I'm sure it was just an old faulty wire, which is what the fire department thinks. Besides, Carol, why would someone want to deliberately set fire to my store? Alice Ann doesn't dislike me that much, does she?" And then she laughed.

George and I looked at each other. Alice Ann? And Paige was laughing? This was too weird. Paige paid the cashier and quickly headed for the exit. As she pulled her car keys out of her pocket, a slip of paper fluttered to the ground. I leaned down and snatched it up. It read: 9-1-14.

"Excuse me!" I called after her. "You dropped this."

She turned back, a startled expression on her face. Then she saw the slip of paper, snatched it from me, and fled without saying thanks.

"Whoa," George said as she appeared at my side. "That was beyond strange."

"Tell me about it," I agreed. We headed back to the checkout line and joined Bess, who was busy loading our groceries onto the conveyer belt.

"What was that all about?" Bess asked.

"Nothing," I said softly, not wanting to speak freely in front of the cashier. Bess gave me a puzzled look, but she just shrugged and began bagging the groceries.

As we headed out to the car, George and I quickly filled Bess in on what she had missed.

"Weird!" Bess exclaimed. "What do you think '9-1-14' means?"

"I don't know," I replied. "A date? It could be some sort of code, though."

"I bet it is a date: September 1, 2014," George stated matter-of-factly.

"Could be," I mused.

We drove back to the cabin in silence, mulling it over. Then we unloaded our groceries and put everything in the fridge, put on our bathing suits, shorts, and tank tops, and headed outside. Bess unlocked the equipment shed near the cabin and retrieved the paddles, while George and I carried the canoe down to the tiny stretch of rocky sand just behind our cabin.

Bess pulled a bright-orange life vest over her head and handed one each to George and me.

"Ugh," she sighed. "Why do they have to make these so ugly?"

"So they can be spotted in a storm," I replied simply.

"Thanks, supersleuth," Bess joked. "It was a rhetorical question, though." She squinted at the sky. "Speaking of storms, it looks a little dark off in the distance, doesn't it?" she asked. "Maybe we should wait until tomorrow to take the canoe out."

She was right—the sky above the horizon was definitely gray. I pulled out my phone to check the weather.

"Well, there's no rain predicted for this afternoon," I assured her. "So I think we should be okay. And I'm really curious to check out Lacey O'Brien's cabin."

George just shrugged and followed us down to the shore. We climbed into the canoe and pushed off. As Bess and I paddled, George sat back and closed her eyes.

I looked at the expanse of sky and the deep-green fir trees that ringed the lake. It should have been relaxing, but it wasn't. I couldn't stop thinking about the fire and the odd facts and timing surrounding it.

"I'm really curious to hear what the fire department says. Paige seemed awfully certain it was accidental, but I'm not so sure. And she was so jumpy when I picked up that slip of paper. And I know she's a recluse, but even though there couldn't have been a signing, I'm a bit surprised Lacey stayed away."

Bess nodded. "Good points."

I continued, "And what about Alice Ann? Even Paige pointed out that Alice wasn't too fond of her."

George glanced down at her phone, which was open to a compass app. "We're here—well, the northwest corner of the lake anyway."

She looked from her phone back up at the sky.

"I'm wondering if maybe we should turn back, though," she said worriedly. "It's gotten a lot darker out here, and my hair's suddenly standing on end because of all the static electricity in the air. I don't like the idea of being on the water in a lightning storm."

"I agree," Bess said nervously. "And the wind is

changing—I can feel it. I'm getting goose pimples on my arms."

The sky definitely did look more menacing than it had before, and the wind had picked up. It was growing increasingly more difficult to paddle through the choppy water. But suddenly, out of nowhere, I caught a glimpse of a dark figure on the beach. Two figures, actually: one in the shape of a bear, the other, a human.

"Look!" I cried out. "Over there. Someone's on the beach."

I gave George and Bess a pleading look.

"We're actually closer to this shore of the lake now than we are to our cabin," George said with a sigh. "I'd rather be near the shore—any shore—than in the middle of the lake if we do run into trouble."

"Maybe . . . maybe we can land on the beach and ask for temporary shelter if it starts to storm," I said.

Bess sighed.

"You're both right," she agreed. "Turning back now in this wind would be more dangerous than going ashore here."

Bess and I paddled hard. The gusts picked up while George gripped the sides of the canoe. The wind started whipping at us from every direction, but there was nothing else to do but press on. If we could make it to the beach, we'd be safe from the storm.

The shadowy figure watched us from the shore. He or she didn't wave or yell out to us. It just watched us struggle. I put my head down and used all my strength as I pulled on the paddle. The waves were getting bigger, and every time one hit us, we rocked unsteadily from side to side.

"Whoa!" Bess cried out.

"Ugh," George moaned. "This rocking motion is making me feel ill."

"Try to keep the canoe cutting through the water perpendicular to the waves!" I called to Bess over the wind. "That way we won't tip over."

"Okay!" Bess called back as she and I both tried hard to turn the canoe so the bow of the boat was slicing through the waves at a right angle. Suddenly the wind changed, and a swell of water hit us hard from the left, causing us to tip toward the right.

"Yikes!" Bess screamed. At that moment George pointed to a floating dock that seemingly just appeared.

"Nancy! Bess!" she shouted. "Watch out!"

In trying not to hit the dock, Bess and I managed to turn the canoe so that we were once again parallel to the waves. A second later we were hit from the left with another giant swell. Before I even realized what was happening, the boat lurched wildly to the right, throwing us into the violent waters.

"Help!" I yelled out.

But my screams were lost in the wind.

CHAPTER FOUR

No Trespassing

I GASPED WHEN I HIT THE LAKE, SUCK-ing down a mouthful of frigid water. Luckily, the life vest kept me afloat as I coughed and spluttered until I had spit most of it out. George and Bess bobbed next to me.

"Are you both okay?" George yelled, wiping a handful of weeds off her face.

"I'm fine," I yelled back as I grabbed hold of the side of the canoe. "Just drank about half the lake, but other than that, I'm okay."

"Ugh!" Bess screamed. She combed a muddy twig

out of her hair with her fingers, and she was covered in lake gunk. She swam around to the other side of the canoe and grabbed hold as well.

I glanced toward the beach to wave for help, but the person who was there before had disappeared. That was strange. Whoever it was had just been there a moment ago. Had the person really watched us capsize and then vanished without offering to help? I was certain since we had also spotted the bear that this was Lacey O'Brien's house.

"Looks like we're on our own," I told my friends. I studied the canoe I was gripping. After we capsized, the canoe had flipped right side up again, only it was now full of water. Then I felt raindrops. So much for getting an accurate weather forecast before we'd set out.

"Hey! Where did that person go?" George asked, incredulous. "What if we were in real trouble out here?"

"Maybe they're going to get help?" Bess said.

George shook her head. "Doubt it," she replied. "Nancy's right—we're going to take care of this. Do either of you have any idea how to empty a swamped canoe?"

I could barely hear her above the wind, and we kept screaming back and forth to one another.

"Well, I did see it in a movie once," I admitted. "First we'll have to dump out most of the water. I guess we'll have to turn it over to do that."

George shook her head. "We're only about thirty yards from shore," she said. "Let's swim in and tow the canoe behind us. We'll wait out the storm on the beach."

Amazingly, we made our way to shore, kicking hard as we towed the boat through the thickening sheets of rain. Luckily, we didn't see any lightning or hear any thunder as we slogged through the lake. It was slow going, but we finally got close enough to the shore so we could stand and dump the water out before we pulled the boat the rest of the way in.

We collapsed on the ground, soaking wet and exhausted. Dragging that canoe was one of the most physically challenging things we had ever done together. Once we were somewhat rested, I stood up, looked around, and saw that the property was covered in NO TRESPASSING signs.

"Not exactly rolling out the welcome mat, right?" Bess commented. "I guess I understand why that person on the beach disappeared."

"Well, I'm not going to let those signs stop me," I replied. "If that was Lacey—or someone else—I want to meet whoever wouldn't help three people stranded on a lake in the middle of a storm."

"And we've got to make it back to our cabin," Bess said, which was something I hadn't actually considered.

The rain had let up somewhat, so George and Bess parked themselves under a tree, while I climbed the wooden steps that led from the shore to the cabin.

I pounded on the back door, waited a good two minutes, and then pounded again. "Hello? Ms. O'Brien?" But nobody came to the door.

When I backed away from the cabin, though, I caught a flutter of curtains at the window beside the back door.

"Hello?" I called out loudly. "Is someone there?

We're just looking for a place to dry off for a few minutes until the storm passes. Hello?"

Still nothing. I waited another minute, but the door remained firmly closed. The curtains didn't move again.

I returned to the beach and to George and Bess. The canoe was emptied, leaning on its side. Just as quickly as the storm had formed, it had let up.

"I thought I saw the curtains flutter when I knocked on the door, but I could have been mistaken," I told them, shaking my head.

"What now?" Bess asked.

"We get back in the canoe and then head back to our cabin," I replied with a shrug. "And we try to figure out why Lacey O'Brien or whoever that was on the beach earlier refused to help us. If that was her, no wonder she has a terrible reputation in town."

George bit her lip thoughtfully. "It was pretty rude," she agreed. "Maybe the fire was set to sabotage her book signing—she may have enemies right here in Avondale."

At that moment, a small motorboat with two men

aboard headed toward the shore. I could see the words AVONDALE POLICE stenciled on the hull.

"You folks okay?" one of the men shouted. "We received a call that a canoe had capsized in the storm. And that trespassers were on this property."

"We're fine," Bess called back. "Just cold, wet, and exhausted."

The boat pulled up to a small dock, and the second officer climbed out. He was much younger than the first and had dark brown hair and eyes. More importantly, he was carrying an armload of thick, heavy blankets.

He walked across the beach and handed one to each of us.

"Thanks!" Bess said, a smile crossing her face. "I haven't been so happy to see a blanket in a long time."

He smiled back at her, blushing slightly and revealing two enormous dimples. The sun peeked out from behind the clouds for a second. Bess lowered her eyes and her cheeks reddened. It was all a little ridiculous, considering what had just happened to us.

George rolled her eyes.

The other officer started talking. "Ladies, I'm Sheriff Garrison. I'm relieved you are all okay, but you must have known how dangerous it was for you to be on the lake with a storm of this magnitude. And trespassing is a serious offense in Avondale. What were you doing here, anyway?"

"The storm came up suddenly and we headed for the nearest shore. Then we tried to get help from the owner of the cabin. We didn't mean to trespass."

"I understand, but the 'No Trespassing' signs are there for a reason. The owner of this cabin likes her privacy and is very wary of any strangers who could be stalking her," said the sheriff.

Bess spoke. "We really didn't mean anything by this, sir. We promise to steer clear for the rest of our visit. I apologize for all of us."

The sheriff nodded. "I will let you off with a warning—this time. But if I hear another complaint about you three, I'll bring you into the precinct. That's a promise."

He walked away and started talking on his phone,

leaving us with the younger officer. We were speechless. How had this weekend taken such a disastrous turn?

He smiled. "I'm sorry my uncle was so rough on you guys," he apologized. "But folks in Avondale really take their privacy seriously. I'm Ian Garrison, by the way. I'm interning over the next couple of months for the sheriff's office. It looks like you could use help getting back to wherever you're going. Right?"

I nodded. "We're heading to our cabin on the southeast corner of the lake," I explained. "I think we'll be fine. But if you're going in that direction, we wouldn't mind the company."

"We're heading that way too. Just consider us your police escort."

"Nancy," I replied as I took his hand. "And that's Bess and George." I pointed to my friends.

"Nice to meet you all," he said.

George and I portaged the canoe down to the shore, Bess carried the paddles, and we climbed in and pushed off. We got back, slowly but surely, the motorboat officers watching our every move.

By the time we got back to our cabin, the weather had cleared. And I couldn't believe it, but it was close to dinnertime. What a day it had been.

"Can we get you anything to drink before you leave?" I asked Sheriff Garrison.

"No thanks," he replied. "I have to get back. But remember, stay out of trouble while you're here." Then he smiled and said, "But barring an emergency, Ian here is done for the day." He gestured to his nephew.

"That would be great, thanks," Ian replied with a shy smile in Bess's direction.

Sheriff Garrison took off, and Bess and I went into the kitchen to get the drinks.

As I sliced some lemons to add to a pitcher of iced tea, I said to Bess, "I was hoping you might be able to pump Ian for some info on the fire." I smiled at her in what I hoped was a winning fashion. "You know, since he seems to really like you."

"He does not," Bess protested. "But I'll ask a few questions if it helps."

We headed back out onto the porch with the ice-filled pitcher, four glasses, and some snacks.

"This is great, thanks. So, where are you all from?" Ian said.

"River Heights," George replied. "We're just up here for the weekend."

"What do you think so far?" Ian asked.

"The lake is beautiful if you can manage to stay in the canoe," I joked. "And we got to check out Avondale earlier today as well. That bookstore fire looked really terrible."

I glanced at Bess to see if she would take the lead.

She turned to Ian and asked, "Who would want to torch a bookstore? We heard some people say that Lacey isn't too popular around here, even though she's a famous mystery writer. And Paige seems to have an enemy or two as well."

"Well, I'm not supposed to discuss ongoing investigations, but we really don't know that much yet. I'm sure it wouldn't hurt," Ian said. "The fire chief and Uncle Bob—uh, I mean the sheriff—were in the bookstore all morning collecting evidence. They still have to evaluate everything officially, but just between us, that fire was definitely not an accident.

"They found traces of kerosene, though they also found some frayed wires on an old chandelier," he continued. "It looked like someone cut through the wires to make it look like that's what started the fire. Now they've launched a full investigation."

So it was official: Someone had started the fire on purpose. But who was the target? Paige? Lacey? Or someone else? I was contemplating my next move when the ringing of Ian's cell phone cut through my thoughts.

"Hey, Uncle Bob," he answered. "Is everything okay?"

The sheriff. It was difficult not to eavesdrop, since Ian was sitting just a few feet away.

"Really?" he asked. "Of course . . . I'll be there as soon as I can."

The call over, he looked at us, seemingly in shock.

"Thanks for the iced tea," he said, nodding his head at Bess as he spoke. "But our small town has been hit again. Someone stole a valuable, one-of-a-kind statue."

He shook his head. "I just don't understand why this is happening."

CHAPTER FIVE

Cracking the Code

BESS WAS UP FROM HER CHAIR IN A second. "Come on, Ian," she offered. "I'll give you a lift back."

George and I walked Bess and Ian to the car. "Do you have any more details?" I asked.

He opened the car door and said, "The piece was by artist Rick Brown. It was taken from one of the small art galleries in town. *The Bride of Avondale*, I think my uncle said."

"Two crimes in less than twelve hours?" George questioned once they drove off. "I know that may not be much for River Heights, but from what we've heard about Avondale, it's pretty suspicious, isn't it?"

"I agree," I said. "I know I've heard the name Rick Brown, but I can't remember where."

"Maybe you saw one of his pieces in a museum, or read about him in art class," George suggested.

"Wait a sec," I said. "I remember." I jumped up and ran into the house to grab the two Lacey O'Brien books I had bought earlier in the day. I came back to the porch and opened one of them to the "About the Author" page and skimmed it quickly.

"I knew it!" I said triumphantly. "I read about the author on the way to the diner before. Rick Brown is Lacey O'Brien's husband."

"That's too much of a coincidence, isn't it?" George said. "I mean, first Lacey's supposed to appear for a reading but there's a fire at the bookstore. Then her husband's statue is stolen from an art gallery on the same day."

I took a sip of tea and closed my eyes for a second.

"Do you remember those two girls at the bookstore fire this morning? One of them mentioned that it seemed awfully similar to the plot of Lacey O'Brien's book *Burned*."

George nodded. "Right," she agreed. "But what does that have to do with the stolen sculpture?"

"Well, *Burned* is about a fire in an old building, and *Framed* is about a theft from an art museum," I told her.

"Seriously?" she said.

I nodded. "And another one of Lacey's mysteries is *Drowned*. Think about what happened to us on the lake before. It sounds like someone's copying the crimes from her mystery novels," I said.

George gave me one of her George looks and said, "Okay, so we could have drowned today in Moon Lake, but why would anyone target us? No one knows who we are. And besides, how could anyone have known we'd go out on the lake and be caught in a storm?"

"But remember Alice Ann—and that waitress— told us where Lacey lives. I just have a feeling it's connected somehow. I know you're beat, but maybe we should start reading *Burned* and *Framed* now.

There just might be more clues to what's next."

"I'll tell you what's next for me, Nancy: sleep. You can wait up for Bess, but I'm going to bed."

The next morning I woke up early and waited to tell Bess and George what I had discovered. I had looked at both books, letting George get her beauty sleep. *Burned* opens with a mysterious fire at an antiques store. The arsonist tampers with the wiring in an old chandelier to make it look as though the fire is accidental. The rest of the plot involves an international ring of criminals who traffic in fake and stolen antiques. The heroine in the novel—a journalist named Lucy Luckstone—breaks the story and eventually solves the case with the help of Detective Buck Albemarle.

The two characters appear again in the novel *Framed*. This time a thief steals a valuable painting from an art museum while Lucy Luckstone is on a behind-the-scenes tour. Lucy is framed for the theft, and Detective Albemarle has to clear her name.

I didn't know if *Drowned* would have revealed

anything helpful, but I didn't have a copy of it.

I was on my second cup of tea when Bess came into the kitchen.

"So, what did you find out?" Bess asked eagerly as she helped herself to a mug of coffee. "Any insight into the Avondale crime spree?"

"Well, I think there's a pretty good chance I'm right about someone borrowing crimes from Lacey's books," I explained. "But I don't even know where to begin in terms of motive."

"How about Alice Ann?" George said as she shuffled into the living room. "You said she didn't seem to like Lacey or Paige all that much."

I nodded. "Could it really be that easy? Who else? Lacey?"

Bess yawned from the couch. "It sounds crazy, but who else knows her books better than the one who wrote them?"

Bess had made a good point. But as much as I would love to talk to Lacey, we had already been warned by Sheriff Garrison to stay away, far way. I wasn't sure if anyone would be willing to talk to strangers from out of town, no matter how friendly people from Avondale appeared.

George looked thoughtful. "Well, you're probably the only person in town who's made the connection between the two crimes," she said. "Ian and the sheriff might figure it out as well, but something tells me you have a leg up on those two, at least for a little while. The sheriff thinks we're stalkers, remember?"

I answered, "I know. But the girls in town did know that the Paige's Pages fire sounded similar to *Burned*. Maybe it would make sense if we let people know about the connection between the two crimes. What do you think?"

George didn't look too happy. "Do we really have to get involved in this, Nancy? Can't we let the sheriff take charge, for once?"

My friends knew me better than that. If there was even a possibility that these occurrences were copycat crimes, then I couldn't ignore them. And it didn't mean they would stop—Lacey O'Brien had written a number of mysteries, and the person or persons behind the fire and the theft had more than enough material to keep them going.

I frowned at George.

She and Bess both sighed. "Okay, Nancy," Bess finally said. "What do we do next?"

I got up from my chair and walked into the kitchen area to pour myself another cup of tea.

"I was thinking I might give Ned and his dad a story for the *Bugle*, and if they want to run it, they would be free to do so."

Bess nodded. "And you'll get this story by . . ."

"Saying I'm a *Bugle* reporter, of course. And that I'm following Lacey O'Brien's rare appearance and book signing in the quiet hamlet of Avondale."

"Hamlet?" George said.

"I'm going to give Ned a call right now," I said. "And then I'll do the dishes. Promise."

My boyfriend, Ned Nickerson, is a part-time reporter and news editor at the *River Heights Bugle*, his dad's paper. The *Bugle* covers a wide area encompassing three counties, including Avondale, so the chances were good that Ned and his dad would be interested in the story.

I quickly filled him in on what had happened yesterday, and he agreed that both crimes sounded newsworthy.

"I'll have to clear it with my dad, but if you write the story, I'll edit it and get my dad to publish," he told me on the phone. "When will you be back in River Heights?"

"I'm not sure. But Bess and George are coming home first thing tomorrow," I replied. "I hope to do the interviews tomorrow morning and write the article tomorrow night so you can post the story ASAP. Sound good?"

"Yes, sounds great," he replied.

After I hung up the phone, I cleaned up the dishes as promised. And because yesterday had been such an unplanned adventure, we decided to relax the rest of the day at the cabin—snacking, napping, reading—before George and Bess took off for home.

After dinner, we decided to play one of our favorite games, Scrabble.

George was easily the best player among us, and

just fifteen minutes into the game, she was well ahead of Bess and me.

"Triple word score!" she shouted gleefully as she played the word ZEBRAS.

"Ugh, and you even have a *Z* in there," Bess groaned.

"Not only that, but the *Z* is on a double-letter-score square," I added with a pained sigh.

"Sorry, girls," George said apologetically, though the smile on her face made it hard to believe she was being sincere.

I played the word YEAR and was left with the letters *A*, *D*, *K*, and *O*. I selected a *Q* and then two *O*s in a row.

"Really?" I exclaimed, exasperated. "Two more *O*s?"

"Nancy, you just totally gave away your letters!" Bess laughed.

I shrugged. I was losing badly by this point anyway. I placed the tiles on my stand with a sigh and started rearranging them. Suddenly I remembered the scrap of paper from yesterday.

"Oh!" I exclaimed, practically knocking my tiles over. "I think I know what that number might have been!"

George and Bess both gave me puzzled looks.

"Number?" Bess asked. "What number?"

"The one on the paper Paige dropped in the supermarket," I reminded my friends.

"What do you think it means?" George asked.

"Well, I was rearranging the letters on my stand, and I was looking at the number of points assigned to each letter instead of at the letters themselves," I explained. "Maybe each of those numbers corresponds to a different letter of the alphabet."

I spun my stand around to show them.

"Well, I guess the game's over if you're showing off all your letters," George joked.

I glared at her.

"Sorry, sorry!" she said, waving her arms in apology. "Please, go on."

"George, I know you thought the number might be a date, but what if it's a word?" I continued. "The numbers were 9-1-14, so we should try the ninth, first, and fourteenth letters of the alphabet."

Bess had been keeping score, so she quickly grabbed a scrap of paper and a pencil and jotted down the numbers one through fourteen on the paper with the letters of the alphabet below them. She studied the paper for a second and then gasped.

"The letters spell the name 'Ian'!" she cried.

"Really?" I asked, intrigued.

"It's a good theory, but why would someone write down numbers instead of letters for someone's name?" George asked. "I admire your sleuthing skills, but maybe the number is just a number."

"You have a point," I admitted. "People sometimes write things down if they're likely to forget them, and 'Ian' doesn't seem like a name that would be hard to remember."

"Or necessary to disguise," Bess pointed out a bit defensively.

"Well, we don't know about that, do we?" George joked. "Maybe he's an undercover spy and his cover is that he's the sheriff's nephew-slash-intern.'"

"Ha, ha," Bess replied, rolling her eyes.

"Wait a minute," I said. "If it is just a number, a number that someone wouldn't want to forget, it could be a combination—maybe to a safe?"

"And that would explain why the bookstore owner looked so alarmed when you picked it up," George pointed out. "Maybe it's the code to a safe she has in the bookstore."

I nodded. "It's a possibility."

"Are we done with this game, then?" George asked as she gestured at the abandoned Scrabble board. "Or are we still playing?"

Bess threw up her hands. "It's no use, George," she admitted. "You'll win anyway. Let's call it quits."

"I agree," I chimed in. "You are truly the champ, George."

With that, we packed up the game and headed to bed.

I fell asleep as soon as my head hit the pillow. But I was startled awake in the middle of the night by a rustling noise outside the cabin. I sat straight up. Bess was still sleeping soundly in the bed next to mine, but I saw George shift in her bed across the room. She sat up too.

I tiptoed over in the dark and perched on the edge of her bed.

"Did you hear that?" I whispered.

She nodded. "It sounds like someone's out there," she said in a hushed tone.

I stood up and dashed back to my bed to grab a sweatshirt and my cell phone—just in case. I pulled the sweatshirt over my head and stepped into my flip-flops. George did the same, and then we quietly went out into the cabin's main room.

A shadow darted past the window next to the front door. George and I both held our breath.

"Maybe we should call the police," she said quietly.

Suddenly the hairs on the back of my neck stood up, and I clutched George's arm.

What I had seen outside was now behind me, but inside.

CHAPTER SIX

Shadowed

THE MOONLIGHT CAST THE FIGURE'S shadow on the wall in front of me. I grabbed a ceramic frog that was perched on the sideboard and whirled around, my heart pounding. I raised the frog, ready to bash the intruder.

"Stop! Don't touch me!" the voice screamed.

Bess?

I lowered my arm. "Bess! You scared the daylights out of us!"

Bess flinched and then scowled. "You almost hit me with that—that ugly frog."

I smiled apologetically. "Sorry," I said sheepishly, glancing at the painted ceramic figurine. "I thought you were an intruder."

"I did too," George added.

Bess glared at us both. "Well, you two are the ones who are out of bed in the middle of the night," she said accusingly. "I heard the floorboards creaking and both of your beds were empty, so I didn't know what was going on. What's up?"

"George and I heard something outside the cabin," I explained, leaning over and flicking on the light switch. "We wanted to check it out."

George nodded. "And then we saw a shadow on the front porch. We were about to call the police when you came up behind us."

"Well, let's call, then. It's possible the intruder is still around." Bess shuddered. "I still don't know why anyone around here is interested in us."

She picked up the phone and dialed 911.

About ten minutes later, Sheriff Garrison appeared at our front door.

"What seems to be the problem, ladies?" he asked. "I didn't expect to see the three of you again so soon."

George said, "We heard a noise outside the cabin. Then we saw a shadow flit across the porch. We thought someone might be trying to break in."

The sheriff looked concerned. "I'm glad you notified us," he replied. "This is the third call we've received tonight from the cabins around Moon Lake. It seems there have been a few sightings."

Bess, George, and I exchanged a look. First a fire, then a theft, our almost drowning, and now three calls to the police in one night? Was that also a plot from one of Lacey's books?

The sheriff's walkie-talkie crackled.

"Unit One, come in."

The sheriff pulled the handset off his belt and replied, "Sheriff Garrison here."

"We're sending the chopper over Moon Lake. Looking for a perp in the southeast quadrant."

"Copy that," the sheriff replied. He turned back to us. "You ladies okay? We're sending the helicopter out over the lake, so if there's anyone still out there, he or she should flee quickly or be caught in the floodlights. In the meantime, lock all the windows and doors and turn on any lights around the outside perimeter of the cabin. I doubt the perp will come back this way, but if you see or hear anything suspicious, just give me a call."

He handed me a card. "This is my cell number. Feel free to call me directly and I'll send someone out ASAP."

"Thanks a lot, Sheriff," Bess replied as she held the door open for him. "And sorry to bother you twice in two days. At least we weren't annoying anyone this time." She smiled.

"No bother," he replied. "That's what I'm here for."

Once the sheriff had gone and we had double-checked to be sure all the doors and windows were locked, we returned to the bedroom and climbed back into our beds.

"Whew," Bess said as she slipped under the covers. "I feel like these two days have been like a roller coaster."

"I know," I said as I lay back against the pillows. "I'm really sorry this visit to Moon Lake hasn't been restful."

I closed my eyes and mulled things over for a few minutes. Could the would-be intruder be connected to the fire and the art gallery theft? I had to check the plots of some of Lacey O'Brien's books to find out if an intruder in the woods was a character who appeared in any of her stories.

I opened my eyes to see that Bess and George were both asleep. I quietly slipped out of bed, grabbed my laptop from my bag, and tiptoed into the living room. Once my computer was running, I did a search on Lacey O'Brien's books. Up came *Framed*, *Drowned*, *Consumed*, *Shadowed*, *Snatched*, *Dragged*, *Ditched*, *Stalked*, *Nabbed*, and *Burned*, with plot summaries of each novel.

I read through the summaries, and my breath caught when I got to *Shadowed*. Lucy Luckstone is the protagonist again, and this time she's spending a week on vacation in a rented cabin on a lake. On the first day of her trip, her wallet is stolen, and for the rest of the week, she feels as though she's being followed. Then one night someone tries to break into her cabin. It turns out she has a doppelgänger who's trying to steal her identity.

My skin prickled. It was as if I was reliving the book. How could that be?

Had I really left my wallet at the Cheshire Cat Inn, or had someone—Alice Ann?—lifted it from my purse and then returned it to me after finding out my background?

I dug through my bag and grabbed my wallet, popping it open to check its contents. My credit card, ID, and cash were still inside. I laughed nervously. Of course Alice Ann hadn't stolen my wallet—she was the one who had brought up my missing wallet when Bess, George, and I returned to the inn, not the other way around. But just because everything was accounted for didn't mean Alice Ann—or anyone, really—hadn't looked through my wallet.

Now I was really being paranoid. But I couldn't

help feeling that I had become the copycat criminal's target.

A wave of exhaustion washed over me. My head hurt from thinking too much about all the different possibilities. I had to get some sleep or I'd never be alert enough to track down the owners of the bookstore and art gallery, and possibly Lacey O'Brien the next morning. With heavy eyelids, I headed back to bed and quickly fell into a deep sleep.

The next morning we were all awake bright and early. George and Bess were packing up to return to River Heights. Meanwhile, I would stay here in Avondale and try to interview as many possible suspects as I could.

I decided to leave our rental cabin on the lake, which, without Bess and George, would be too isolated for me to stay in alone. I thought I'd stay in town at the Cheshire Cat. I'd be able to keep my eye on Alice Ann and anything else that happened.

"Nice to see you again, Nancy," said Alice Ann as she checked me in. "So glad you decided to stay here after all. I think Two-B would be perfect for you. Just up the staircase, second door on your right."

Two-B was decorated with everything related to famous writers, from Edgar Allan Poe to Emily Dickinson. A bust of William Shakespeare sat on the night table, and a framed needlepoint of the Robert Frost quote, "Two roads diverged in a wood, and I—I took the one less traveled by," hung on the wall above the bed.

There was even an old typewriter on a desk in front of the windows. I looked for a memento of Lacey O'Brien, but there was nothing honoring her in the room. That would be odd, if I didn't already know Alice Ann's true feelings about her.

I headed to Paige's Pages bookstore first. It was still closed, of course, but I was hoping Paige might be around cleaning up after the fire. The store was locked up tightly, though, and there was still police crime-scene tape across the front door.

I headed around to the back of the store, where a woman with dark, graying hair in a messy bun was loading large trash bags into a white pickup truck. I recognized her immediately as the woman from the grocery store—Paige.

I cleared my throat softly and she whirled around, clutching her chest.

"Oh!" she exclaimed. "You scared me. Can I help you?"

"My name is Nancy Drew, and I'm on assignment for the *River Heights Bugle*," I introduced myself, holding out my hand. "Are you the owner of the bookstore?"

She studied me carefully, taking in my notebook, sunglasses, and reddish-blond hair.

"Have I met you before?" she asked, genuinely perplexed. "Have you been to my store?"

I figured she might recognize me from the grocery store, and it seemed like the best thing to do was just fess up.

"I think our paths crossed at the grocery store on Saturday," I admitted. "You dropped a slip of paper and I handed it back to you."

She smiled.

"Oh, yes, of course," she replied. "Thank you for that. And I apologize if I was abrupt. I was a bit out of sorts that day, with the fire and everything. I still am today, I'm afraid. I didn't sleep much last night."

She wiped her hair out of her eyes with the back of her hand, and I noticed the dark circles under her eyes. Then she said, "I know the investigators said it may be arson, but who would do such a thing? We're a quiet town, with law-abiding citizens. This is quite disturbing."

I thought back to my busy night and didn't blame her for not being able to sleep much, given what she had been through.

She took my hand and shook it firmly. "I'm Paige Samuels," she said.

"I realize it must be difficult, but I'd like to speak with you for a few minutes about the fire," I explained. "I'm doing a story about a few crimes that have taken place around town over the last few days."

"A few crimes?" she asked, her eyebrows raised. "I didn't know there were others."

I nodded. "There was a theft in town Saturday as well, and sightings of an intruder near Moon Lake last night. I think the crimes may be related. Do you have a minute to talk?"

Paige nodded. "Let me just put this last bag of trash in the back of my truck and then we can grab a coffee at the diner. The firefighters let me bag up some debris on Saturday before they began their investigation. I figure there's still plenty more to do inside the store, but for now, I may as well clear away as much of this trash as I can."

"No problem," I said. "Should I meet you there in about fifteen minutes?"

Paige nodded. "Sure, that works."

I got back in my car, drove up the street, and parked in the lot across from the Avondale Diner. Standing on the curb, I quickly glanced to the left and right before stepping into the crosswalk.

Suddenly a black car raced around the corner, tires squealing, heading straight for me!

CHAPTER SEVEN

Close Call

THE CAR SWERVED TO THE LEFT JUST as I jumped to the right, landing in a planter full of impatiens. The flowers managed to cushion most of my fall, though my right thigh was somewhat scraped and bruised from where it hit the edge of the planter.

Slowly I stood up, and as I brushed myself off, I saw that the black car had screeched to a stop and pulled over to the curb ahead. A man and a woman got out and approached me hurriedly. The woman was tiny and wore an oversize hat and sunglasses. The man, in a dark, ill-fitting suit, was extremely tall. Both were pale and looked completely shocked at having come so close to hitting me. The woman grabbed both of my hands and looked me straight in the eyes.

"Are you okay?" she asked a bit hysterically, her voice rising in pitch at the end of the question.

I nodded. I was a bit shaky, but I was otherwise fine. I hadn't even torn or dirtied my shorts, despite the scrape on my thigh. *Wait until Bess and George hear about my latest brush with death,* I thought. *They'll never believe it happened in Avondale.*

The woman turned to the man and poked him in the arm, hard.

"I told you to slow down, Rick," she shrieked, almost in tears. "You almost ran this woman over. You could have killed her!"

"I know, I know," he lamented, wringing his hands.

He turned to me. "Words cannot express how sorry I am, and how thankful I am that you're okay," he said genuinely.

"It's all right," I replied, giving them both what I

hoped was a reassuring smile. "I'm fine, really. It was clearly an accident."

"Do you need us to call an ambulance or the police?" he asked.

"No need for that," a loud voice replied from behind me. "The police are already here."

I turned to see Ian and Sheriff Garrison heading toward us.

Oh no, I thought. Not another encounter with the Avondale police! This was getting a bit absurd.

Sheriff Garrison interviewed the couple and me and took down a full report, while Ian tended to my leg using a first aid kit that looked like it was at least ten years old.

"Are you sure that adhesive is still sticky?" I joked as he placed some gauze over the scrape.

"Are you kidding?" he replied. "They don't make this stuff like they used to. I'll bet this will still be stuck to your leg a year from now."

Once Ian was done patching me up and Sheriff Garrison had completed his report, I assured everyone for the tenth time that I was just fine. Then the woman reached into her purse with shaking hands and pulled out a small notebook. She wrote down a phone number and address, tore the sheet out, and handed it to me.

"We're on our way to an appointment outside of town, but please call on us later today if you need anything at all," the woman said.

I glanced at the slip of paper before putting it in my pocket.

"Sure, thanks," I replied, though I doubted I would ever call. I had a full day planned, and though I was still a bit shaken, I was fine.

The couple climbed back into their car and drove away, and Ian and the sheriff turned to me.

"Are you sure you're all right?" Ian asked yet again.

"Of course!" I replied, smiling reassuringly. "You did a great job patching me up."

"I'm going to stop by the cabin later this afternoon, if that's okay," Ian told me. "You know, just to make sure."

I smiled. "Since Bess and George went back to River

Heights, I checked into the Cheshire Cat Inn. It's not necessary, but that's where I'll be if you want to stop by."

I waved a quick farewell and hurried across the street to the diner. Paige was waiting for me at a windowed corner booth.

"Are you okay? I just saw that car almost take your life," she said.

I smiled sheepishly. "Really, I'm fine. No worse for wear," I said as I settled in across from her and began the interview.

"What can you tell me about the fire Saturday morning?" I asked as I opened my notebook. I would have taped our interview, but thought I would be less threatening just taking notes.

"Well, we had a book reading and signing scheduled for ten a.m. with Lacey O'Brien. We're not particularly close, but we were in the same class in high school. Once a year, I'm able to convince her to come out for a special event. Well, her husband convinces her. I knew him back then too. They're high school sweethearts, you know."

She paused and looked off in the distance distractedly for a moment before she continued. "Of course, as you know, the event never happened. When I showed up at eight to open the store, the firefighters were already there. It looks like the blaze broke out in the early morning, and the firefighters think it was caused by old electrical wiring."

I jotted everything down in my notebook.

"I thought the firefighters were investigating the possibility that the fire was caused by an arsonist," I pointed out. "Isn't that why there was police tape up around the store?"

Paige sighed heavily. "I was hoping you wouldn't have to print that in your article," she explained. "The bookstore hasn't been doing too well lately, and I didn't want the bad publicity. But you're right—the sheriff and the fire chief are investigating the matter. I hope it wasn't arson and that the fire was accidental."

I nodded as I made a few more notes, thinking back to what Ian had said about the sheriff and the fire chief finding the kerosene and frayed wire in the bookstore. Clearly Paige was in denial about the cause of the fire. "Ms. Samuels, if it was arson, do you have any idea who would want to torch your shop?"

"Please, call me Paige," she said. "Oh, my. Absolutely not. As I said before, this is a very small town, and everyone here gets along."

Hmm, I thought. *Not exactly.* I thought of Alice Ann, and how she didn't seem to care much for either Lacey O'Brien or Paige. I still found it hard to believe that Alice Ann was behind the fire or the theft, but stranger things had happened. But I still couldn't figure out what her motive would have been. And was it Alice Ann who'd been on the porch of our cabin? If it was, she sure knew how to cover up her feelings, as she couldn't have been nicer to me when I got a room at the inn.

I caught Paige glancing at her watch, so I quickly moved on to the next topic.

"Did you call to tell her about the fire?"

Paige nodded. "After I'd spoken with the firefighters, I did call her to let her know what happened.

We briefly discussed rescheduling the appearance for later in the year, after the store reopens."

"And her husband, Rick Brown. Do you know him well?" I asked.

Paige shrugged. "Not really. Like I said, we went to high school together, but that was ages ago."

"You do know that one of his sculptures was taken?" I said.

"I just heard about it on my way here," Paige answered. She shifted in her seat and glanced at her watch again.

"For the life of me, I don't have a clue as to who would be targeting Avondale's fine arts," she said. "Books and paintings and sculpture are important tourist attractions for us and add so much to our community. I do hope the police get to the bottom of this and fast."

She paused, then said apologetically, "I should probably be getting back. I have so much cleanup work to do."

"Of course," I answered. "Just one last thing. Some

people have theorized that the arsonist and the art gallery thief may be perpetrating crimes based on some of the plotlines in Lacey O'Brien's books."

Paige looked startled. "Really?" she asked. "You mean, like a copycat criminal?"

"Exactly," I explained with a nod. "Do you think you could help me contact Lacey? I'd like to speak with her about her books, but I know she's reclusive. I'd also really like to interview her husband about his art piece."

Suddenly Paige's face lit up.

"Did you happen to catch the names of the couple from your accident?" she asked.

I thought back to the police report the sheriff had filled out, wondering what this had to do with Lacey O'Brien.

"I think they were Richard and Cecilia Brown," I told her. "Why?"

She leaned in and whispered, "Well, the couple that tried to run you down was none other than Lacey O'Brien and her husband!"

CHAPTER EIGHT

The Secret Door

I PULLED THE SLIP OF PAPER THE woman had handed me earlier out of my pocket. It read:

555-0192

34 Crescent Lane

"Cecilia Brown is Lacey O'Brien?" I asked, incredulous.

Paige nodded. "Lacey O'Brien's been her pen name since we were in high school," she explained. "She always hated the name Cecilia Duncan. She was named for her grandmother, and Lacey thought it sounded old-fashioned. It didn't help that most of the kids in school called her CeeCee, even though she despised the nickname. She almost always goes by Lacey these days, but it makes sense that she gave her real name to the sheriff."

"But he acted like he didn't even recognize her," I said. I couldn't believe that the sheriff hadn't known that Cecilia Brown and Lacey O'Brien were one and the same person.

Paige shrugged. "He probably didn't," she said. "Most folks in Avondale have only heard of her as Lacey O'Brien, the local mystery writer, and don't know her personally. Aside from her close friends and people who grew up with her, not many local residents would recognize her. I only know her real name is Cecilia because of our high school days. So it's no surprise the sheriff didn't know who she was. He's only been in office a few years, anyway."

I glanced back down at the slip of paper. What luck! As crazy as it sounded, almost getting hit by a car was turning out to be my best break of the day. I was all but guaranteed an interview, or at the very least, a meeting with the famous author later that afternoon.

For now, I had one more place to visit in town—the art gallery.

"Thank you again for your time," I told Paige. "The story should be in both the online and paper edition of the *River Heights Bugle* tomorrow morning."

"Of course," she replied. "I'm happy to help. And thank you for looking into the fire. If it was arson, I'm eager to find out who's behind it."

"Me too," I assured her. "And I won't stop investigating until I do."

Paige offered to pay for our coffees on her way out, and I headed to the ladies' room.

On my way there, I realized someone was in the booth right behind ours. Oddly, he or she—I really couldn't tell—was hunched down in their seat and seemed to be hiding behind a large menu. But I was able to glimpse a shock of curly brown hair with a streak of gray.

"Alice Ann?" I asked tentatively.

She lowered the menu and seemed surprised to see me there. An empty coffee cup and a plate with the remains of a slice of pie sat on the table in front of her. Since I hadn't seen her come in, I figured she had been there the whole time Paige and I had been talking, which meant she had likely heard our entire conversation. And considering she was my number one suspect—maybe my only suspect—I wasn't thrilled that she was pretty much spying on us.

"Nancy!" she replied a bit too cheerfully as she jumped up and grabbed her check from the table. "I didn't know you were here."

She waved the bill in front of me as she headed for the cashier.

"In a hurry!" she cried. "I've got to get back to the inn!"

I walked out the door, shaking my head. In addition to being one of the town's biggest gossips, it seemed Alice Ann was also an expert eavesdropper. Or was it more than that? I thought back to the wallet incident on Saturday. Was it possible that Alice Ann was really shadowing me? I was glad that my stay at the inn would keep her close to me.

I headed outside, and after quickly checking directions on my phone, I realized I could walk the few blocks to the art gallery. I glanced behind me a few times on the way just to be sure Alice Ann wasn't tailing me. I was fairly confident I was on my own, but I felt jumpy all the same. I couldn't shake my suspicions about that woman.

The Clancy Tate Gallery was cool and bright, though the scene that greeted me was anything but cheerful. A thin, tight-lipped man in a dark turtleneck and thick glasses with tousled hair was standing in front of a desk in the corner, having a heated argument with a woman in a blue suit standing opposite him.

"Mr. Tate, please, I ask you not to raise your voice!" she implored him. "I assure you that it won't help the situation."

The man sat down in his chair abruptly and slumped back, looking completely dejected.

"I'm ruined!" he wailed.

"Now, now, Mr. Tate," the woman replied in a clipped voice. "There's no need to be so dramatic."

The man stood back up and squared his shoulders proudly before he addressed her again.

"Excuse me," he began softly. "But you've just come into my gallery and informed me that my insurance policy lapsed three days ago, and that no one from your agency had the decency to send me a renewal notice. So for the last three days—including the day before yesterday, when a valuable piece of artwork was stolen from this gallery—I have had absolutely zero insurance coverage! Which means that I am solely responsible for the cost of the piece! And you dare to accuse me of being overly dramatic?"

He was shouting loudly by the end of his brief speech.

The woman retreated sheepishly.

"I do apologize, Mr. Tate," she replied. "Perhaps I should come back tomorrow so that we can discuss this further."

She turned to leave and saw me standing near the entrance.

"And I see you have a customer as well, so I'll be out of your hair now," she said as she quickly darted past me and out the door.

The man sighed loudly.

"Thank goodness that vile woman is gone," he muttered, more to himself than to me.

Suddenly he seemed to notice me standing there.

"Oh, excuse me," he apologized, a dazed look on his face. "Can I help you?"

"I hope so," I replied. "Are you Clancy Tate?"

He grimaced. "I'm afraid so."

"My name is Nancy Drew," I introduced myself. "I'm on special assignment for the *River Heights Bugle*, investigating the recent Avondale crime spree. Would you have a moment to answer a few questions about *The Bride of Avondale* for my article?"

"Would I?" Mr. Tate asked. "If your article can help get the statue back, then I've got all the time in the world."

We sat at a glass-topped table, and once again, out came my notebook.

"When did you first notice that the sculpture was missing?" I asked.

"I was the only one here. One of my co-workers had the day off and another called in sick." Mr. Tate paused and then went on. "Lacey O'Brien's fans were in town for her signing at the bookstore. I guess a few of her 'super fans' know she's married to the sculptor Richard Brown, so they came flooding in to see one of his most beloved works. It's not a large piece—in fact, it's rather delicate—but the detail and intricacy is meticulous.

"We had about twenty more people than usual sign the guest book on Saturday. At one point, I must admit, I did go in back to look for a sepia photograph of Moon Lake by Ethan Jenkins, another of our local artists." He took a deep breath and continued. "After that, I was busy making a sale of a few posters to a woman from Louisiana. When I realized the statue was gone, I called the police immediately, and they were here within minutes. But it was too late. The thief was long gone—it could have been anyone."

"May I see the guest book?" I asked. I didn't think a thief would actually sign in, but I still had to check.

"Go right ahead," Mr. Tate replied. He handed me a thick, oversize leather book and opened it to the most recent page.

I scanned down the list of names and addresses. A few were locals, but most of the addresses were from neighboring towns. Ian Garrison . . . the sheriff's nephew? Arnold Edwards . . . was that the man in the apron talking to Alice our first day? But one name stood out more than the others: Alice Ann Marple.

Hmm. If Alice Ann was the thief, she was either the dumbest thief in the world for signing the book or incredibly shrewd.

"Do you mind if I take note of these names and addresses?" I asked.

"No, not at all," Mr. Tate replied. "Like I said, if your story helps get that statue back, I'll be in your debt forever. And you know what they say about publicity— it's never a bad thing, at least in the art world. Do you want me to make a copy of that page for you?"

"Nope, I've got it," I replied. I used my cell phone to take a photo of the register before I handed the book back to him. I started to put my notebook away, when Mr. Tate cleared his throat.

"There's one thing I forgot to mention, and it involves Lacey O'Brien. But I can only tell you off the record. It would be a security risk for me if you printed it in the paper."

I was immediately intrigued.

"Of course," I assured him. "From now on, everything you say is one hundred percent off the record."

"There's one other way to get into the gallery. Only a few people know about it. I mentioned it to the police, and they've concluded that's probably how the thief came in and exited."

"Go on," I prodded. I sure wished Bess and George were here. I could have used some extra eyes and ears.

"The gallery actually shares space with a mystery writers' retreat and workshop," he explained. "As a wealthy local artist, Richard Brown has always been a huge investor in and supporter of the gallery. A few years ago Lacey had the idea to fund a dedicated writing space for fledgling mystery writers. She and Richard didn't want their names attached to it, since she so closely guards her privacy. But Lacey still believes beginning writers should get a break, especially mystery writers."

Gee, I thought. That didn't sound like someone who thought she was better than everyone in town.

Mr. Tate went on. "Anyway, Richard proposed closing off the back half of the gallery that faces Oakwood Lane and turning it into the writers' space. There would be a separate entrance, and Lacey would rent the space from me. She and I are the only two people with a key to the door between the gallery and the writers' space."

My mind raced as I quickly processed the new information.

A place just for writers? Mystery writers? Even though Lacey didn't want anyone to know the space was her brainstorm or that she was paying for it, I wonder if she ever dropped in as her "former self," Cecilia Duncan. Most people probably wouldn't guess that their writing mentor or coach was the bestselling Lacey O'Brien. It was as if she was hiding in plain sight.

Whoa—besides Mr. Tate, Lacey was the only person with access to the gallery through the secret entrance. But why would she have stolen her own husband's sculpture? Was it some sort of strange publicity stunt? As Mr. Tate had said, no publicity is bad publicity in the art world—or the world of publishing.

"Who owns *The Bride of Avondale*?" I suddenly asked Mr. Tate.

"Lacey does. I put it on exhibit to coincide with her book signing."

"Wait a minute, the sculpture that was stolen was one of Lacey O'Brien's, and she's the only one—other than you—who has access to the gallery through a secret entrance?" I asked.

At that moment a crash sounded from a back room. Could Lacey be in the writers' room now?

A voice called out, "Sorry, Uncle C. I was standing on a stool in the supply room and lost my balance." Into the gallery walked a girl with a familiar-looking face.

"Mandy!" I said. "What are you doing here?" It was the girl who was with her friends the other day, standing outside Paige's Pages after the fire.

Mr. Tate asked, "Do you two know each other? How can that be?"

Mandy looked at me quizzically at first and then had a "lightbulb" moment of recognition. "Hey, you're the person who was asking me and my friends Carly and Rachel all about the bookstore."

"That's right. I'm Nancy Drew. I'm writing an article about the recent crimes in Avondale and have been interviewing Mr. Tate about the theft of the statue," I explained.

"Well, my uncle C is totally clueless about it," she said. "But I think someone is definitely lifting their ideas from Lacey O'Brien's books—just like I said the other day. And my friends and I think it might even be Lacey O'Brien."

I might not have thought Mandy knew what she was talking about the other day, but right now we were on the same page.

CHAPTER NINE

Framed

I RAN OUTSIDE AND CALLED GEORGE, quickly updating her on what I had discovered. "What do you think?" I asked.

"I don't buy it," George said. "It's just too, I don't know . . . convenient."

I agreed. I didn't actually believe Lacey had stolen the statue either, but clearly she had to be considered a suspect.

George continued, "Since the statue was just on loan to the gallery, Lacey doesn't have a real motive for stealing."

"You're right," I said. "The motive question is definitely a problem. But that doesn't change the fact that she had ample opportunity."

"But it's all so obvious," George replied. "It's almost as if someone chose stealing the sculpture because it would make Lacey a prime suspect."

"Exactly! Lacey's being framed, just like the character Lucy Luckstone in her novel *Framed*."

"That makes sense," George answered. "Kind of. Do you think she's also being set up with the fire? Who would want to frame her, Nancy?"

I kept walking down the street and noticed the Avondale Library. I sat down on a bench in front to continue our conversation.

"I understand those crimes could be connected to Lacey and her books, but what about the intruder at our cabin, and the canoe, and me almost being run over?" I asked her.

Nothing answered me.

"Hello? George? Are you still there?" I asked.

George spoke. "Nancy, when were you almost run

over? Are you okay? See what happens when Bess and I aren't around to chaperone you?"

Oh no . . . I'd never told them about my near accident. "I'm fine. Really. But because of it, I'm hoping to get a face-to-face meeting with Lacey O'Brien."

George laughed a bit on the other end of the phone. "Only you, Nancy, only you could have that happen. But nice work. If you need us to come back to Avondale, just say the word."

We hung up, and I walked back to my car. Instead of first calling Lacey, I decided to drive right to her house. Maybe by surprising her I would get more information. Or perhaps a confession?

I used my phone's GPS to navigate from town back to Moon Lake and 34 Crescent Lane. Lacey and Richard's cabin was set back from the road, covered, it seemed, by giant oaks and pine trees. I pulled into the long driveway and in two minutes was knocking briskly on the front door.

Within seconds, Cecilia Brown—aka Lacey O'Brien—flung open the door and greeted me by grabbing both of my hands tightly in hers and squeezing them, hard.

"Please tell me you're still feeling okay, dear," she gushed as she swiftly pulled me into the house.

"Of course!" I replied. "I'm feeling just fine. Honest."

Her cheeks reddened, and she looked down at her feet in what seemed to be embarrassment.

"I'm afraid I owe you an apology," she said softly. "I know who you are."

Wow. Did she know I was writing an article? And that I suspected her of staging her crimes from her books?

She continued, "I recognize you from the lake on Saturday. You had two other young women with you. I'm so very sorry Rick and I didn't come out to help you. I truly regret it. It's just that—well, we've had people stalk us from Moon Lake in the past, and we're never sure who to trust."

Lacey wrung her hands nervously, then said, "We did call the sheriff, but there's still no excuse for our not coming out there ourselves to make sure you were okay."

I was stunned. That Lacey—Cecilia—was so honest and forthcoming took me by surprise. Could this truly be someone masterminding a local crime spree?

"Thank you, Mrs. Brown," I answered. "Luckily, we were just drenched to the bone, shaken up somewhat, but nothing more serious."

"Why don't we sit down and make ourselves comfortable," she replied, and I followed her into a warm and comfortable living room, with floor-to-ceiling windows overlooking the lake. We settled in on an overstuffed couch.

"We were not stalking you, but we did hear that this is where Lacey O'Brien lives. And when you and I had our run-in in town, I had no idea you were Lacey O'Brien."

I paused and then admitted, "I'm not here about our run-in this morning, though. I'm here because I'd like to interview you for an article I'm writing for the *River Heights Bugle*."

Again, Lacey looked embarrassed. "I see it wasn't hard for you to connect the dots about who I am. I'm so sorry, but I don't grant any interviews about my work," she explained. "I made a decision many years ago not to allow interviews, so now I'm afraid I'm stuck. If I make an exception for one paper, the floodgates would open. I hope you understand."

Once again, she seemed genuinely sorry.

"The story isn't about your writing," I said. "It's actually about a number of crimes that have taken place around Avondale this weekend."

"What does that have to do with me?" she asked, looking me squarely in the eyes.

Truth time. I was a little nervous to directly confront Lacey and was hoping she wasn't currently writing a mystery entitled *Murder at Moon Lake*, but I had to take the chance. I probably should have looped in Sheriff Garrison and Ian, but I kind of knew they wouldn't approve of what I was doing.

"My article reports the ways the perpetrator of the crimes is stealing ideas from your books—*Burned* and *Framed*. The police and the fire department have determined that the bookstore fire started due to wiring in an old chandelier that had been tampered with—exactly like what happened in *Burned*. And besides Mr. Tate, you're the only one with a key to the gallery's back room and easy access to the statue. I'm afraid that you're at the top of my suspect list."

Lacey paled. And then grew angry.

"That's awful," she said. "And, frankly, I resent your accusations. However, for your information, I was home the morning of the fire—Paige called me to tell me about it. I certainly couldn't be two places at once!"

She went on heatedly, "There is no way I could be your culprit."

I exhaled. What a relief.

"Now I'm the one to apologize, Lacey. But I hope you understand that I had to play my hunch," I said.

There was somewhat of an awkward silence before I spoke again.

"It's quite possible then that you're being framed."

"Me, framed?" She laughed lightly, and I realized

it was the first time I had seen her smile. But then she paused as though trying to determine whether she should reveal something.

"About ten years ago a big fan of my work called me every day. He figured out where I lived and trailed me around town for a number of weeks. He was basically harmless, but I ended up getting a restraining order because it was very unsettling. The last I heard, he had retired to Florida and was doing well. That's the main reason Rick and I became so reclusive and protective of our privacy. We didn't want to go through something like that again," she said.

"Have you heard from him recently?" I asked.

"No, I haven't," she replied with a shake of her head. "I actually have no reason to suspect him, but we do have a history, so it's one possibility."

"Anyone else?" I said.

She shook her head again. "I'm afraid there's no one I can think of."

I took down the former stalker's name anyway. Though it didn't sound like a promising lead, I intended to look into it. Then I gave her my number and asked her to call if she thought of anything else. "If anyone comes to mind, please let me know. Who knows what they'll do next to set you up?"

"I'll definitely be in touch if I think of anything," Lacey said. "Nancy, I should let you know that I'm going to tell my husband Richard what's transpiring. I don't want either of us letting down our guard."

She walked me to my car and warned me to be careful.

"I know Avondale has a peaceful facade, but one never knows what lies beneath."

Even though it was warm outside, Lacey's words chilled me to the bone.

Another exhausting day. I drove back to town, looking forward to the quiet of my room at the inn. Now I had to write the article, and by the time I was done with it, I realized I hadn't solved a thing and had actually created more questions than I had answered.

Just after seven thirty, I hit send with my article to

Ned. Then I called to let him know it was on its way.

"You sound beat, Nancy," Ned said. "Maybe I should drive to Avondale tomorrow and help you out."

"I'm fine. If I can't figure this case out in the next two days, I promise to turn it over to the sheriff," I told him. I was about to hang up, when there was a knock at my door.

"Hold on a minute, Ned. Let me see who this is." I padded past the Dr. Seuss chair and opened the door.

Nobody was there.

But on the ground was an envelope with my name. I opened it, wondering what it could be, a thin slip of paper fluttered out. I picked it up and read the type-written note:

STOP PRESSING YOUR LUCK. IF YOU KNOW WHAT'S GOOD FOR YOU, YOU'LL GET OUT OF TOWN NOW.

CHAPTER TEN

Stalked

"NED, I'LL CALL YOU RIGHT BACK," I SAID, and hung up.

I peered at the note and realized it had been typed on an old-school typewriter rather than printed out from a computer. I looked at the letters closely and realized that all the *T*s were more faded than the other letters, as though that key on the typewriter didn't work quite so well.

I looked up and down the hallway and didn't see or hear a soul.

Suddenly my phone rang, and I jumped. "Hello? Who is this? What do you want?"

"Nancy? It's me, Ned. You said you'd call back in a minute—what happened?" He sounded panic-stricken.

"Ned! I'm sorry—but I think I will take you up on your offer. Can you come to Avondale first thing tomorrow?" I said.

"Of course I'll come. But are you all right tonight?" Ned asked.

I assured him I would lock my door, not open it for anyone, and meet him at the Avondale Diner at eight a.m. We said good night and I got into bed, still tired and now a bit scared.

Not surprisingly, I had trouble falling asleep. A million thoughts filled my head. I must have been closer to who was behind this mystery than I realized. Who'd left that note, written with a typewriter?

I sat up in bed. Typewriter . . . there was one right on the desk in my room. I turned the night table lamp on and walked over to the desk. I took a sheet of the Cheshire Cat Inn stationery and put it in the roller.

I typed the same words in the note: STOP PRESS-
ING YOUR LUCK. IF YOU KNOW WHAT'S GOOD FOR YOU,
YOU'LL GET OUT OF TOWN NOW.

I ripped out the paper, inspected the *T*s, and almost
started crying, but from relief: This wasn't the same
typewriter used to write the note sent to me. I'd been
so worried that someone had snuck into my room. But
maybe, just maybe, if I found the typewriter that was
used for the letter, I would find out who was behind
the crimes.

The next morning I was already on my second cup
of tea, reading my article in the *River Heights Bugle*,
when Ned arrived at the diner. He listened closely while
I filled him in on everything that had happened—
everything I hadn't written about in the article, that
is—over the last few days.

"So you've talked to Paige, Lacey, Alice Ann, and
Mr. Tate. It could be any of them, Nancy," Ned said.

It was great seeing Ned. And great to be able to
bounce theories off him. After we talked, we both were

in agreement about two things: We didn't think Lacey was the culprit. And in order to find who was, we had to find the broken typewriter.

I figured we'd swing by Paige's Pages first, and then stop at the Cheshire Cat Inn. Both seemed to be likely spots for an antique typewriter. But the bookstore was dark and the web of police tape still decorated the front door. I cupped my hands around my face to block out the bright sunlight and peered inside, but the store looked deserted. I realized I didn't know how to reach Paige other than by stopping by the shop, but then I remembered Alice Ann. Maybe she would be able to tell me where to find the bookstore owner.

"Nothing?" Ned asked as I backed away from the darkened window.

"Nope," I replied, shaking my head. "Let's walk up the street to the Cheshire Cat Inn. Wait till you see this place."

When we entered the inn, Alice Ann was front and center behind the receptionist's desk, chatting with someone on the phone. When she saw me come in, her face lit up. She gestured that she would be just a moment, and I nodded before Ned and I ducked into the gift shop.

"Wow, she sure has a thing for cats," Ned remarked as he took in the array of cat-shaped knickknacks crammed into the tiny space.

"Mm-hmm," I replied absently as I surveyed the space for typewriters. Antiques and old-looking memorabilia were everywhere. My eyes took in a shelf of antique scissors (strange items for an inn gift shop, I thought) and old-fashioned writing devices like fountain pens and quills. In addition to the spinner rack of paperbacks that housed all of Lacey O'Brien's books, there was a shelf of dusty old dictionaries, encyclopedias, and Avondale High School yearbooks. But there was no typewriter.

"Nancy!" a voice cried out behind me, and I turned to see Alice. Shockingly, she grabbed me and gave me a friendly hug.

"Oh!" I exclaimed. "Hi, Alice. Good morning."

She laughed. "I hope you had a restful night. I was looking for you this morning, but you were out bright and early. But now I can thank you in person."

"Thank me?" I asked, genuinely perplexed. "For what?"

"Ever since your article was published in the *River Heights Bugle* this morning, my phone has been ringing off the hook," Alice replied, a huge grin on her face. "We've had a tough summer at the inn, and it's been hard to book rooms. But it seems that people all over the county are curious about Avondale and Moon Lake since your story came out. We're completely booked for the next three weekends, and I imagine we'll be full for the rest of the summer by the end of the day. It seems people want to make a weekend trip to Avondale so they can retrace the steps of the copycat criminal. And relax by the lake, of course."

"That's a little disturbing," Ned replied, a troubled look on his face.

"Well, yes, I suppose it is," Alice admitted, and her brow wrinkled for a moment in dismay. Then she shrugged. "But it's been great for business."

At that moment the phone rang again, and Alice dashed back to the reception desk to answer it. Ned and I continued to browse the shop while she finished the call. About fifteen minutes later she returned.

"Sorry about that," she explained a bit breathlessly. "Now, what can I do for you two?" She studied Ned carefully and raised her eyebrows questioningly at me.

"This is Ned Nickerson," I replied. "Ned, this is Alice Ann Marple."

"Very nice to meet you," Alice said as she shook his hand.

"You too," Ned replied. "Nancy told me about your little shop, and I know how much she loves antiques."

"Actually, I was really looking for an old-fashioned typewriter," I jumped in. "Would you happen to have any of those?"

I watched her closely to see her reaction, but Alice Ann barely blinked.

"No, I'm afraid not," she replied. "But I do have some vintage typewriter ribbon tins. They're very collectible." She pointed to a shelf of colorful lidded tins.

I shook my head. "But who buys the ribbons without the typewriter?" I asked. "I was really hoping for a typewriter. I couldn't recall whether you had one in here or not."

I smiled, and Alice did as well. She didn't seem rattled at all when I mentioned looking for a typewriter.

"You might try Memory Lane on Oakwood," she suggested. "Stephen Grey is the owner, and he might have something like that in stock. Just tell him I sent you."

"Okay, thanks," I replied. "I appreciate it."

"It's no problem at all," Alice Ann gushed. "I really am so grateful for your article. Not that I'm pleased about the crimes that have taken place, of course," she added, her face growing serious. "I hope you don't think I'm an opportunist like all these tourists who have been calling this morning."

"No, no, not at all," I murmured.

"I mean, I'm not at all happy about the reason I'm

seeing so much new business. It's just that the inn has been struggling so much recently I've thought about throwing in the towel and retiring early. But this new business should be enough to keep us afloat at least through the end of the year, which is when we usually see a bump thanks to the ski resort in nearby Sugarville."

"I understand," I told her. "Don't worry, we don't judge you."

"Well, thank you," she replied, her cheeks reddening a bit. "I'm a little embarrassed to be profiting from the crimes, but what can you do? It is what it is."

Ned and I nodded in agreement. Truthfully, I did agree with her. If she hadn't committed the crimes, then it wasn't her fault that was the reason tourists were flocking to the Cheshire Cat.

"Well, thanks for your time," I told Alice as we headed for the door. "Oh, one more thing. Any idea where I can find Paige Samuels? I wanted to ask her when she thought the bookstore would be reopening and if she was going to reschedule the Lacey O'Brien signing."

"Really?" Alice Ann replied, looking more than a little curious. "Well, she often has lunch at the diner, so you might try to find her there. Or you can swing by her place. She lives in an apartment on Oakwood Lane, right above the antique shop, in fact."

Alice prattled on. "I don't know where she's been keeping herself. I know the fire put her store out of commission for a time, and she's probably mad as blazes at Lacey . . . for so many reasons dating back to high school that I couldn't even begin to tell you about, but, no, I haven't seen her."

"Thanks, Alice Ann," I said. I was grateful when the phone rang and Alice Ann stopped gossiping.

Ned and I headed out into the warm morning.

"Well, she sure is something," Ned said softly as we left the inn. "Doesn't want to profit off the crimes, huh?"

"How can't it be Alice Ann?" I whispered to him. "We've got a motive now—her business was suffering and now it's booming. She doesn't particularly like Lacey or Paige, either." I paused. "But we still need actual proof. We've got to find that typewriter."

Ned nodded.

As we walked past my car, he plucked a piece of paper from the windshield and held it out to me. "Hey, what's this?" he asked.

Oh no! Not another note. Again, it was typed in all caps:

MS. DREW: YOU SEEM TO HAVE TROUBLE

FOLLOWING DIRECTIONS. DON'T SAY I DIDN'T WARN

YOU. . . .

CHAPTER ELEVEN

Opportunity Knocks

MY STOMACH DROPPED TO MY FEET. Who was watching me?

"There goes that theory," I said with a shudder. "There's no way Alice Ann could have put that note on my car; she was with us the entire time. And we just passed my car on our way from the bookstore to the inn."

I chewed my lip as I thought things over. Then I glanced down at the latest note again. I needed to find that typewriter—it was our best clue. And I was worried about what would happen next . . . to me, or someone else in Avondale.

"Let's go to Memory Lane, then," Ned suggested. "Maybe the owner knows of someone in town who's a collector."

"Sounds like a plan," I agreed, giving him a grateful look. "Thanks again for coming along today."

"Happy to help," Ned said, reaching over and giving my hand a squeeze. "You'll get to the bottom of this. I just know it."

A few minutes later I parallel parked in front of Memory Lane. There was a doorway just next to the entrance that had two buzzers. The top one was labeled SAMUELS. I rang and waited a minute or so before ringing again. When there was no response after the third ring, I gave up, and Ned and I headed into the antique store.

The shop was dim, dusty, and absolutely crammed from floor to ceiling with antique furniture, light fixtures, candlestick holders, china, cameras, and clocks. Ned and I made it about two feet before we were stopped by an enormous antique bookshelf filled with crumbling old books. We couldn't figure out how to get around it, so instead I called out for help.

"Hello, Mr. Grey?" I cried. "Is there anyone here? We could use some—uh—assistance."

"Coming, coming!" a muffled voice replied from what sounded as though it was somewhere below us. A minute later a man with horn-rimmed glasses popped up behind me.

"Hello! So sorry to keep you waiting," he said. "I was just in the basement organizing some stock. What can I do for you?"

"Alice Ann Marple sent us over. We're looking for any old or antique typewriters you may have."

He scratched his head and looked around at the piles and piles of stuff surrounding us.

"Typewriter . . . typewriter," he muttered. "Let me check my inventory. Come right this way."

Mr. Grey darted to the right and squeezed his way past the enormous bookshelf. Then he weaved his way through a row of wicker chairs and around a mirrored door that was leaning against the wall until he came to a rolltop desk that was completely covered in more paper. He picked up a large notebook and began to thumb through pages that were covered in rows of nearly illegible scrawls of ink.

"Ah, yes!" he exclaimed, pointing at a row in his ledger. "We do not have a typewriter."

"Uh, okay," Ned replied, glancing at me. *How is this helpful?* he mouthed.

I just shook my head at him. *Trust me,* I mouthed back.

"Does that mean you used to have one but it's been sold?" I asked.

"Indeed it does," Mr. Grey said with a nod.

"That's too bad," I replied, thinking quickly. "Did you happen to sell it to someone local? I'm a collector and would pay top dollar."

Ned raised his eyebrows at me. *Nice,* he mouthed.

"Of course, of course," Grey replied without hesitation. "I sold it to that famous writer. What's her name again? Lacey O'Neil? She was wearing a big hat and sunglasses so I wouldn't recognize her, but I knew who she was."

He shook his head before he continued, "That typewriter wasn't even in very good shape. In fact, there were a few keys that were broken when she bought it."

Ned and I looked at each other and quickly said good-bye. I grabbed his hand and hurried him out the door. "We've got to question Lacey again—come on, we're driving to Moon Lake."

I was glad to leave the dust and papers behind and be outside in the sunshine.

"One more second, Ned. Let me ring Paige's buzzer again. Maybe she came home while we were talking to Mr. Grey," I said. But Paige still wasn't home, or just not answering. We started to go to my car when I noticed the storefront on the other side of Memory Lane. It was unmarked, but there was a logo of a quill and a jar of ink etched into the glass door. That had to be the writers' space that was connected to the art gallery. We didn't have time to check it out—we had to get to Lacey.

I was sorry that Ned and I couldn't enjoy the

scenery or a hike as we drove out to Moon Lake.

Right before we pulled into her driveway, Ned asked, "What about Lacey's stalker? Did you check him out? These notes seem to have 'stalker' written all over them. No pun intended."

I had to smile at Ned. I knew he was trying to calm my nerves. "I did check up on him. I placed a few calls before you came this morning and confirmed that he's still in Florida."

We got out of my car, and it took all my self-control not to run to the porch. I rang the bell and we waited. I rang again, willing Lacey to be home.

Finally the large oak door opened. Lacey looked at me like she didn't recognize me. But an instant later she exclaimed, "Nancy! It's lovely to see you again so soon. Is everything all right? Have you found the guilty party?"

But I wasn't as warm and friendly to her. "May we come in, please? This is my boyfriend, Ned Nickerson."

"Please do. Come in and have some tea," Lacey

said. "Rick's in his studio working, but I'll go get him."

Just like yesterday, Lacey didn't act uncomfortable or guilty in the least. Ned and I sat down in cushy green armchairs in the living room, while Lacey disappeared into the back of the house. She returned a few minutes later with a tray of tea and her husband.

"Nice article, Nancy," Rick remarked as he shook my hand. "Are you any closer to solving this mystery and recovering the stolen statue?"

"Rick!" Lacey scolded him. "Isn't clearing my name more important?"

"Of course," he replied. "But I'm sure that finding that statue will clear your name."

He turned to Ned and me. "The sheriff and his assistant were here earlier today with a search warrant. They were looking for the sculpture."

I looked at Lacey expectantly.

"Of course they didn't find it, because it's not here," she told me. "But they're getting a warrant to search my writers' space next."

As Lacey fixed herself a cup of tea, I took out the

typewritten notes I had received. I took a deep breath and began.

"I know you were adamant yesterday defending yourself. But not only did someone make sure I got these notes"—I paused and held them up—"but we found out from Stephen Grey that you were the one who bought the typewriter they most likely were written on."

Lacey and Rick exchanged glances. "May I see those, please?" she asked. She took the papers and slowly read the messages.

"I didn't write these notes!" she exploded. Her face turned red.

I held my breath as I waited for her to explain.

"The typewriter is at Oakwood Writers' Workshop, of course," she replied. "But no one uses it. It's there merely as decoration. And perhaps inspiration for the writers. You must know, Nancy, that hardly anyone uses typewriters anymore."

I nodded. "True. But anyone who uses the space had access to the typewriter and to the secret entrance to the art gallery."

"No one has access to the art gallery through that entrance except Lacey and Clancy," Rick chimed in.

"For both your sakes, I really hope you're wrong about that," I said.

Again, Rick and Lacey glanced at each other. What was in that look? Did they seem concerned about something? Maybe I had been right about Lacey's innocence, but could Rick have been involved?

"How can we help?" Rick asked.

"I think Nancy really needs a list of people who are members at Oakwood," Ned suggested helpfully.

I nodded.

"Just give me a few minutes and I'll print the membership list from my laptop," Lacey said.

The next five minutes seemed to take an eternity.

When Lacey returned with the sheet of paper in her hand, I jumped up from my chair. I scanned the list from top to bottom three times. One name made me stop—and I realized I had to get back to town, now.

CHAPTER TWELVE

❧

The Final Clue

I DIDN'T WANT LACEY—OR RICK—TO know I suspected anyone on the list, so I handed it back to her and thanked her.

As they walked Ned and me out, Lacey told us about a last-minute fund-raiser that they were holding tonight at Mr. Tate's art gallery. With the theft of the *Bride of Avondale* statue, his gallery was in jeopardy of closing because of the lapsed insurance policy, and the local art community had organized the event.

Rick glanced at me and said, "You and Ned should come. Lacey and I will get you tickets. And you can ask your friends who had the canoe mishap the other day to come as well. It's the least we can do."

"Thank you," I answered. "We'll try to be there."

Once we were in the car, I turned to Ned. "We've got to hurry," I told him. "We have to get back to the Cheshire Cat Inn and then to that fund-raiser!"

"The Cheshire Cat?" Ned looked at me, incredulous. "But it can't possibly be Alice Ann—you said so yourself!"

"Trust me on this one," I said. "There's something there that I need. Let's go!"

I drove carefully but quickly, hoping Alice Ann hadn't locked up the gift shop for the day. I figured she was attending the fund-raiser that evening too, and she probably needed some time to get ready. As I drove, Ned called Bess and George to see if they could make the trip to Avondale in time for the fund-raiser. I figured Ian would be there, so it wouldn't be hard to sway Bess, but I wasn't so sure about George.

"Neither of them answered their phones, but I left messages," Ned said.

"Perfect," I replied. "Hopefully they'll be able to make it."

We drove the rest of the way in silence as I puzzled over all the clues. I was pretty sure I had figured out who was behind the crimes, but there were still a few loose ends that needed tying up.

"Penny for your thoughts," Ned said, breaking the silence.

"You'll know soon enough," I replied.

Before I knew it we were back in town. I parked in the lot behind the inn and hurried inside, Ned struggling to keep up with me.

I slipped into the dark lobby and headed straight for the gift shop, almost crashing into Alice Ann as she turned the key to lock the door to the tiny room.

"Wait!" I cried. "Don't lock up just yet. Can you let me back into the shop?"

"Nancy?" Alice Ann asked. "Whatever for? I'm running late for a fund-raiser at the Clancy Tate Gallery."

"I know," I replied. "I am too. But first, there's

something in your shop that I need to borrow, just for the evening."

"Borrow?" Alice Ann asked, raising her eyebrows. "This isn't a library, you know. People tend to buy the things they like, especially if it's something to wear to a fancy event."

"It's nothing like that," I explained. "I need to look at your Avondale High School yearbook collection. I'm this close to solving the mystery of the bookstore fire, the art gallery theft—oh, everything!"

Alice Ann smiled brightly.

"Well, why didn't you say so?" she asked. "In that case, go right in."

She unlocked the door and pushed it open, practically shoving me inside. Then she flicked the lights back on and hustled me over to the bookshelf where I had seen the yearbooks earlier that day.

"Which one do you need?" Alice Ann asked. "And I knew you weren't just a reporter working on a story— you're really a detective, aren't you?"

"Well, yes," I replied. There was no sense keeping

up my cover story when I was this close to solving the case and knew that Alice Ann wasn't who I was after. "I am. And right now I'm really hoping you have the yearbook from the year you graduated. That's the year that Paige, Rick, and Cecilia graduated too, right?"

"Yes, that's right," Alice Ann replied, a puzzled look on her face. She pulled a dusty book off the shelf. "Here it is. But our high school days were years ago. I really don't see how that's going to help you," she said.

Suddenly I had a pang of doubt. What if I couldn't find the proof I was looking for? What if the hunch I had was just that—a hunch?

Alice let me take the book back to my room, and she closed up the shop. Back in room Two-B, I sat down on the Dr. Seuss chair and began flipping through the yearbook.

"Who—or what—are you looking for?" Ned asked, looking over my shoulder.

"Pictures of Rick Brown," I replied.

I turned a page, skimming captions of sports teams and school clubs. But finally I found him: an image of

Rick in a tuxedo, standing arm in arm with a pretty girl with curly hair in a lovely, off-the-shoulder evening gown.

I had never been so happy to see an old prom picture in my life!

Luckily for Ned and me, the Clancy Tate Gallery fund-raiser wasn't a black-tie affair. Since it had been planned at the last minute, everyone was dressed casually, so we didn't stick out too much in our khakis and sneakers.

It was wall-to-wall Avondale when we walked in. In just a few days, I already recognized faces, from Alice Ann to Lacey to Paige and even Mr. Tate and Mandy. It seemed like there was a great deal of support for Mr. Tate and his gallery.

I knew that the fund-raiser was the perfect cover for me to finally get to the back writers' room. I would try to convince Mr. Tate to give me the key so I could look around for myself.

"Ned, you stay here and mingle," I told him. "I'm going to talk to Mr. Tate alone."

But I couldn't get close to him with the all the people who were listening to his story of the statue's theft.

I walked to the rear of the gallery, to the locked door to the writers' space. I wanted to will it open and wished there was a magical phrase like "open sesame" that would somehow make it so.

But something magical did happen: The door opened and out walked Mandy.

"Mandy! What are you doing here?" I started to shriek, but quickly lowered my voice. "I mean, what are you doing in there?" and motioned my head toward the door.

"Hi, Nancy." Mandy smiled. "I had to escape this crowd. Really, how boring can it get? People just telling Uncle C how wonderful they think this boring gallery is, over and over again," she said. "I couldn't stand it."

"But I thought only your uncle and one other person had the key to this door. Was it left unlocked?" I asked.

"Unlocked? No," Mandy answered. "The writers'

room isn't a secret to me. I know where the key's hidden, so I take it anytime I want. Like I said the other day, my uncle is pretty clueless. Nice, but clueless." She laughed a little bit.

And then she said, "I hang out here a lot. Sometimes with my friends, sometimes with the writers. Ms. Samuels is even there right now."

"Paige? Paige is in the room?" I said.

Mandy nodded and then took off. So I slowly, quietly opened the door and couldn't believe my eyes: Paige was there, just as Mandy had said. And in her hands was *The Bride of Avondale*!

"Sheriff Garrison," I screamed. "HELP!!!"

CHAPTER THIRTEEN

~

Facing the Facts

PAIGE TURNED AROUND AND GASPED.

There stood not only me, but Sheriff Garrison, Ian, Ned, Lacey, Rick, Mr. Tate—and what seemed like the entire population of Avondale.

"Ms. Samuels, just what do you think you're doing?" asked the sheriff.

"I'm—I'm—," she sputtered.

"Caught red-handed, I'd say," Lacey said, and walked into the room.

I thought Paige was going to pass out, but instead she placed the statue on a shelf—right next to an old typewriter—and then she sat down at one of the writer's desks.

"I'm sorry," she began. "I didn't mean for—"

Sheriff Garrison interrupted her. "Stop right there, Ms. Samuels. You have the right to remain silent."

And then he and Ian walked calmly over to the owner of Paige's Pages and escorted her to their police car.

One week later Bess, George, and I were sitting in my kitchen, having apple pie and chocolate butterscotch cookies—just the treats we were craving.

George took a sip of lemonade and said, "So Sheriff Garrison was ready to arrest Lacey O'Brien for the crimes? The 'intruder' at our cabin turned out to be a bear—that's what he said, right? See, Bess. I told you he and Ian needed help. It's a good thing Nancy was there."

Bess rolled her eyes but smiled at her cousin. "And Paige was so jealous of Lacey's success and her marriage to Rick. But still, to go to those lengths?"

I sighed. After Paige's arrest, Alice Ann had actually visited her in jail. I don't know if she went just to find out more gossip or to finally be a friend, but Alice found out that Paige had always felt she was competing with Lacey, as far back as high school. But she never came out ahead—even though she had attended the prom with Rick. That's the photograph I saw in the old yearbook.

When the bookstore started doing poorly, Paige planned to close it. But then she devised a plan to make money from the insurance company—an idea taken straight from Lacey's mysteries. The fire was meant to look like an accident. But once she realized that the fire and police departments suspected foul play, she started to cover it up.

I took my plate to the sink and let the water run over the leftover crumbs.

"I think there was a part of her that wanted to get caught," Bess added. "Why else would she join the writers' space and hide the statue in her own locker? She was bound to be found out, especially after getting the writer's room key from Mandy."

Bess had a good point. I wondered whether, when I'd picked up the paper with her locker combination on it at the grocery store, Paige had been deliberately dropping clues.

"Well," I told my friends, "I'm glad no one got hurt. Broken hearts, maybe, but nothing else. And now I've got one more mystery for you to solve."

George groaned. "Please, Nancy. Say you're joking. How much more can we take?"

I started to laugh. "Where do you think I put the latest Lacey O'Brien mystery? I can't find the book anywhere!"

Dear Diary,

A few months later, Ned and I took a day trip to Avondale. We had read that Lacey and Rick Brown bought the bookstore—now called Brown's Books—and completely renovated it, expanding the mystery and children's sections.

And inspired by the town's new notoriety, Alice Ann began hosting Murder Mystery weekends at the Cheshire Cat Inn to continue to draw new tourists. I hear they're a smashing success. But as far as I'm concerned, I think I've had my fill of mysteries at Moon Lake.